"You're afraid."

Caleb stepped closer to her—so close Portia could smell the dizzyingly familiar scent of him.

His words gave the tense feeling inside her a name. Fear.

"It's creepy to think that somebody could possess this much hatred toward me."

Caleb reached out and touched her chin. "It could be kids looking for a little excitement. If that's the case, somebody will talk to somebody else and eventually I'll hear about it."

"I hope you're right," she said, wishing he'd pull her into his arms and hold her, take away the chill that refused to leave.

And for just a minute she thought she saw in his eyes the desire to do just that.

Dear Reader,

I love a good reunion story where two people who got it wrong the first time around have an opportunity to try to get it right. I especially like stories about high school sweethearts who meet years later and still have the magic between them.

In my family we have one of those stories. Several years after the death of my father-in-law, my mother-in-law reconnected with her first love. They hadn't seen each other since they had been teenagers, but the magic was still there.

At the ages of eighty-four and eighty-eight, they married and have had five beautiful years together so far.

It's been ten years since the hero and heroine of this book were high school sweethearts, and a crime has brought them back together again. There is still some magic between them, but the only question is, will it be a killer or their pride that might ruin any second chance at happiness?

Hope you enjoy!

Carla Cassidy

CARLA CASSIDY

The Lawman's Nanny Op

ROMANTIC
SUSPENSE

SILHOUETTE BOOKS

Recycling programs for this product may not exist in your area.

ISBN-13: 978-0-373-27685-1

THE LAWMAN'S NANNY OP

Copyright © 2010 by Carla Bracale

This edition published by arrangement with Harlequin Books S.A.

For questions and comments about the quality of this book please contact us at Customer_eCare@Harlequin.ca.

® and TM are trademarks of Harlequin Books S.A., used under license. Trademarks indicated with ® are registered in the United States Patent and Trademark Office, the Canadian Trade Marks Office and in other countries.

Visit Silhouette Books at www.eHarlequin.com

Printed in U.S.A.

Books by Carla Cassidy

Silhouette Romantic Suspense

*Man on a Mission #1077
Born of Passion #1094
*Once Forbidden... #1115
*To Wed and Protect #1126
*Out of Exile #1149
Secrets of a Pregnant Princess #1166
**Last Seen... #1233
**Dead Certain #1250
**Trace Evidence #1261
**Manhunt #1294
†Protecting the Princess #1345
†Defending the Rancher's Daughter #1376
†The Bodyguard's Promise #1419
†The Bodyguard's Return #1447
†Safety in Numbers #1463
†Snowbound with the Bodyguard #1521
†Natural-Born Protector #1527

A Hero of Her Own #1548
†The Rancher Bodyguard #1551
5 Minutes to Marriage #1576
The Cowboy's Secret Twins #1584
††His Case, Her Baby #1600
††The Lawman's Nanny Op #1615

*The Delaney Heirs
**Cherokee Corners
†Wild West Bodyguards
††Lawmen of Black Rock

CARLA CASSIDY

is an award-winning author who has written more than fifty novels for Silhouette Books. In 1995, she won Best Silhouette Romance from *RT Book Reviews* for *Anything for Danny*. In 1998, she also won a Career Achievement Award for Best Innovative Series from *RT Book Reviews*.

Carla believes the only thing better than curling up with a good book to read is sitting down at the computer with a good story to write. She's looking forward to writing many more books and bringing hours of pleasure to readers.

To Ann and Bruno,
for finding love again after all these years.

Chapter 1

Four cartons of crayons, a ream of construction paper, ten glue sticks and a dozen boxes of tissues. Portia Perez smiled to herself as she pulled up in front of the discount store.

Her best friend Layla West would think it was pathetic that Portia's shopping list didn't include a pair of three-inch red heels and something skimpy and sparkly, but Layla had never spent eight hours a day entertaining twelve little kids.

As the owner and operator of Portia's Playpen, a day-care facility, Portia would much rather have enough crayons and glue sticks than shiny high heels any day.

As she got out of her car, the hot, early-morning

August air felt like a slap in her face. There were times she didn't think the sun shone any brighter in any other town on earth than it did in August in Black Rock, Kansas.

The concrete pavement beneath her sandals already radiated with heat and she reminded herself to add a couple of tubes of sunscreen to her shopping list.

She was almost to the store when she saw the first flyer. It hung on a light pole and as she glanced at it she froze. Her own face stared back at her.

"What the heck?" She moved closer to read it and as she did her heart banged hard in her chest and all her breath whooshed out of her body. *Portia Perez—Baby Beater and Child Abuser. If You Love Your Kids, Don't Use Her Day Care.* The words swam before her eyes, for a moment making her nauseated.

She yanked it from the pole and then looked down Main Street, stunned to see more flyers on other poles. Shopping forgotten, she hurried down the street, taking down the flyers as she fought against the angry tears that threatened to erupt.

Who would do this to her? Who would be so cruel? This wasn't just cruel; it was criminal. Somebody was trying to destroy her business, her very livelihood.

It took her fifteen minutes to take down all the flyers she saw in the immediate area. She held them in a trembling hand and stared across the street at the sheriff's office.

She needed to report this. It was slander at its worst. Surely Sheriff Tom Grayson would do something, find the person responsible.

Who could be behind this? Her head whirled as she marched across the street and into the sheriff's office. The minute she opened the door and stepped inside the tension that already coiled tightly in her stomach increased as she saw who sat behind one of the desks.

Deputy Caleb Grayson.

For almost ten years of her life Portia had gone out of her way to avoid any real interaction with the man. In a town the size of Black Rock they'd had occasions to run into each other, but any conversation had been polite and impersonal.

It amazed her that after all these years just the sight of him created a faint twinge in her heart. But she couldn't think about that now. She had more important things on her mind than an old heartbreak.

"Portia," he said in obvious surprise and stood from the desk.

"Is Tom in?" she asked.

"No, it's his day off. What's up?" He stepped closer to her, close enough that she could smell the scent of his cologne, a familiar scent that would always remind her of high school prom and things she'd never wanted to think about again.

"This is what's up...up all over town." She handed him one of the flyers.

He frowned as he read it aloud. "Portia Perez neglects and abuses your children that you put in her care. Portia's Playpen is a place of pain for little ones without a voice. Don't let this woman watch your kids." He whistled low beneath his breath and looked at her once again. "You've apparently made somebody very mad."

"You have to do something," she exclaimed. "They're everywhere, each one more slanderous than the next."

"Did you see who posted them?" he asked.

"No, but it's...it's all lies." Once again she felt the pressure of tears welling up, but the last person in the world she would cry in front of was Caleb Grayson. "I want whoever did this arrested."

"Unfortunately this is more of a civil matter than a criminal one," he replied. "I'll ask around, see if anyone saw somebody putting them up, but there's really nothing more I can do."

It wasn't what she wanted to hear. In fact his apparent lackadaisical attitude about the whole thing irritated her. She wanted him outraged on her behalf. She wanted him out beating the streets to find the guilty and she wanted that person lynched at high noon in the hot sun.

More than anything she wished Caleb wasn't so darned handsome. She wished that his shirt didn't stretch so neatly over his broad shoulders, that his slacks didn't hug the length of his long legs and that that lock of his dark brown hair on his forehead didn't look as if it were begging for female fingers to gently push it back into place.

"You'll call me if you find out who did this?" she asked curtly.

"Yeah, but I wouldn't wait by the phone if I were you. These were probably put up sometime in the middle of the night and I doubt that anyone saw who hung them."

"So that's it?" she asked, not attempting to mask her anger.

Caleb shrugged. "Sorry, there's not much else I can give you."

Portia whirled around on her heel and left the office without another word. Still stunned by the flyers, irritated that she had to have any dealings with Caleb Grayson, she stalked across the street and down the block to Black Rock Realty.

Even though it was early, Layla would be in and Portia needed to talk to somebody who would be properly outraged and lend support. Her best friend since childhood would do just that.

As she entered the office Layla looked up from her desk with a smile. "Hey, girl, what are you doing in town so early? Most Saturdays you aren't even dressed until noon."

"I came to pick up some supplies. Take a look at these." Portia threw the flyers on the desk then flopped down in the chair facing her friend.

Layla scanned a flyer then looked up at Portia, her green eyes wide. "Where did you get these?"

"They were taped to light poles around the discount store."

Layla looked back at the piece of paper in her hand. "But who would do something like this? Have you had a fight with any of the kids' parents?"

"No, nothing like that. I can't think of anyone who would have a reason to put them up."

"What are you going to do about it?"

"I already did it. I marched myself into the sheriff's office."

"What did Tom say?" Layla twisted a strand of her long blond hair between two fingers.

Portia frowned. "Tom wasn't in. I had to talk to Caleb."

Layla raised a perfectly formed blond eyebrow. "And how did that go?"

"He told me it was a civil matter, not a criminal one. I think he just didn't want to be bothered with the whole thing. He probably couldn't work my crime into his busy schedule."

Layla smiled at her knowingly. "Now that wouldn't

be a little ancient history aggression coming into play, would it?"

"Don't be ridiculous, I don't harbor any ill will toward Caleb. What happened between us happened a long time ago. I've certainly moved on since then."

"Yeah, right, and I'm going to be six feet tall when I wake up in the morning," Layla replied dryly. "Admit it, you've carried a torch for Caleb Grayson ever since high school."

"That's the most outrageous thing you've ever said," Portia exclaimed.

"Really?" Layla dropped the strand of hair she'd been twisting. "You think it was more outrageous than that time I told you I had sex with Ralph Davidson in the front of his pickup and my hip bumped the shift knob so we ended up in his pond?"

Portia laughed, which she knew had been Layla's intention all along. "You're crazy," she said.

"And that's why you love me." Layla leaned forward and covered one of Portia's hands with hers. "Don't worry about the flyer nonsense. Everyone in town knows those kids at your day care are your life and you'd never do anything bad to any of them."

"I hope you're right," Portia said.

Layla grinned. "Of course I'm right. I'm always right. Now get out of here. Go buy your supplies. I have a client due to arrive any minute and I'm hoping to schmooze him into buying the old Miller property."

"That old dump?" Portia said as she stood.

Layla grinned. "By the time I finish with my sales pitch my client will think it's Buckingham Palace."

Portia was still smiling as she left the realty. Layla was always good for cheering her up no matter what the circumstances.

Of course, that whole thing about Caleb and a torch was utterly ridiculous. If she had a torch and Caleb came too close to her, he'd definitely get burned. She'd given him not one, but two chances years ago, and he'd blown them both.

"Fool me once, shame on you. Fool me twice, shame on me," she muttered as she headed to the store to pick up her supplies.

Caleb Grayson was as much a part of her past as teenage blemishes and pep rallies. She'd outgrown all of them, most of all the very hot, handsome Deputy Caleb Grayson.

He dreamed about her Sunday night. A wild, hot dream that combined part past and part fantasy and woke him with a yearning he hadn't felt in years.

Caleb Grayson pulled himself out of bed Monday morning, irritated that Portia Perez had invaded his sleep in any way, shape or form. Minutes later, as he stepped into his shower, he tried to shove thoughts of her out of his head, but they kept coming.

She'd been his first love and he'd never loved like that again. A year ago he'd thought he'd finally found love with Laura Kincaid, but that had ended so badly he still felt a burn of anger when he thought of her. A swell of grief threatened to sweep over him, but he consciously shoved it away and instead focused back on Portia and her current problem.

The flyers had been a nasty piece of business, but he'd spent most of the morning on Saturday asking around to see if anyone had seen who'd posted them and as he'd suspected, nobody had a clue who might be responsible. There wasn't much else he could do about the situation.

Stop thinking about her, he commanded himself as he got dressed in his khaki uniform. Besides, all the Grayson men had more important things on their minds than ugly flyers hung around town.

Their sister, Brittany, had been missing for almost five weeks. Caleb strapped on his gun and grabbed his keys from the kitchen table and tried to still the thundering in his chest that began whenever he thought of his younger sister.

She'd disappeared the week of the sixth anniversary of their parents' death and for the first two weeks or so Caleb and his brothers Tom, Benjamin and Jacob had just assumed she'd gone off alone to get through the difficult anniversary. But too much time had gone by without any of them hearing from her.

His brother Tom, the sheriff of Black Rock, had been doing what he could to find some answers. He'd issued a BOLO alert on her vehicle and was monitoring her bank account and credit cards. There had been no sign of her car anywhere but what was more troubling was that her accounts hadn't been touched since the day of her disappearance.

This wasn't the first time Brittany had disappeared, but before it had always been only for a few days, a week at the most, then she'd turn up with explanations and apologies.

Caleb knew all his brothers felt the same as he did, that they didn't care about apologies or explanations; they just wanted to know that she was okay.

He got into his car and headed for the office. Caleb lived in a small rental house in the heart of the small town of Black Rock. He'd moved there seven years ago from the family ranch when he'd gotten the job as deputy when he turned twenty-one.

Law enforcement in Black Rock was definitely a family affair. Tom was the sheriff, and Caleb, his brother Benjamin and his sister, Brittany, were deputies. His brother Jacob had been an FBI agent, but had returned home almost two months ago and shut himself up in a small cottage on the ranch property.

He refused to talk about what had brought him home and didn't want anyone except family to know he was there. It was bad enough when Caleb just had Jacob to worry about, but now he had Brittany, as well.

No wonder he couldn't get Portia out of his head.

She was the least of his worries. Despite the fact that they shared the same town, he rarely saw her.

Still, there had been a moment yesterday when she'd first stepped into the office when his heart had done a little dance in his chest.

"Indigestion," he muttered as he pulled up in front of the two-story brick building that was his home away from home. Surely that was all that he'd felt when he'd seen Portia.

It was only a few minutes before seven in the morning but already the sun was warm on his shoulders as he got out of the car.

"Good morning, Sam," he said as he entered the office.

Deputy Sam McCain gave him a sleepy smile and raised his coffee cup in greeting. "Coffee's fresh and I brought in some homemade cinnamon rolls that Loretta baked this morning."

"You're a lucky man, Sam," Caleb said. "Not only is your wife gorgeous, but she cooks, as well."

Sam's teeth flashed white against his cocoa-colored face as he grinned. "You stay away from my Loretta. You with your legendary charm might turn her head."

Caleb laughed. "You know I save my charm for the single women in town. Besides, for reasons I can't understand, Loretta seems to be madly, crazy in love with you."

Sam chuckled. "Yeah, I can't explain it, either."

At that moment the phone rang and Sam answered. Instantly his broad forehead creased in a frown. "Okay, all right. We'll get somebody right over there."

He hung up the phone and looked at Caleb. "That was Portia Perez. Somebody broke into her day-care center last night."

"I'll go," Caleb said. "First those flyers and now this. I wonder what's going on?"

Minutes later he was in his car and headed to Portia's place. She lived on the north edge of town, not far from the house where she had spent her childhood.

Caleb had spent many nights of his high school years visiting Portia and her mother. In fact, he and Portia had been inseparable all through high school.

On warm summer nights he'd sat on the porch swing with Portia and they'd talked about their future together, made plans for a lifetime of happiness. They'd been best friends, and on the night of their senior prom they had become lovers.

He thought of the dream of her he'd had the night before. It had been hot and wild and when he'd finally awakened he had imagined he could smell the scent of her still lingering in the sheets, on his skin.

Crazy, he thought. Crazy that after all these years she should invade his dreams. And just as crazy that the thought of her could still bring the taste of bitterness to the back of his throat.

Her house was a small ranch, painted the color of cinnamon and with gingerbread trim in beige that gave it a fairy-tale look. Colorful flowers lined the sidewalk leading up to the front door and baskets hanging from the porch ceiling spilled blossoms of red and purple.

He turned in to her driveway and followed it to the detached garage where he knew her day-care facility was housed.

As he pulled up he noticed several things. Melody Markfield, Portia's assistant, was in a fenced play area next to the building with several toddlers, and Portia stood at the front door, her face unusually pale in the early-morning sunshine.

He parked the car and as he opened his door to get out, she approached him. He couldn't help but notice the way the sun sparked on her copper-colored hair and that her legs beneath her denim shorts were just as shapely as they'd been when she'd been a cheerleader in high school.

"What's going on?" he asked.

"Somebody broke in." Her voice trembled slightly and her hazel eyes appeared larger than usual. Her chin tilted upward. "And if you tell me this is a civil matter I might just punch you in the stomach."

"Let's take a look inside," Caleb said. As he walked toward the door of the building he was conscious of her just behind him. The floral scent of her perfume eddied in the air and reminded him of his dream of her.

But all thoughts of dreams fled from his head the moment he stepped into the day care. Destruction and vandalism were everywhere.

The mattresses on two of the cribs had been slashed and the stuffing pulled out. Books had been thrown from shelves and toys had been smashed and littered the floor in colorful plastic shards.

"Not civil, definitely criminal," Caleb murmured as he walked around the room and tried to take it all in.

He checked all the windows looking for a point of entry and finally found it in the small bathroom. The window had been broken inward and pieces of glass glittered on the floor in the sunlight.

He left the bathroom and returned to the main room. A laptop computer sat on the adult-size desk in the corner, along with a stereo system, letting him know that robbery hadn't been the intent.

It was a malicious crime scene. Whoever had broken in had been hell-bent on causing damage and nothing else. Who would have done this and why?

He turned to look at Portia, who leaned against one wall with her arms wrapped around her waist. Her eyes held the hollow look of someone who had taken a hard hit to the head and wasn't quite sure where she was or how she had gotten there.

"When was the last time you were out here?" he asked.

She raised a hand to her temple, as if she had a headache. "Last night. I came in around six to make sure everything was ready for this morning and then I went back into the house." Her voice still held a faint tremor.

"And you didn't hear anything out here?"

She shook her head. "Nothing."

"Do you have any idea who might be responsible for this? Have you had a fight with somebody? Maybe one of the parents of one of the kids?"

She shook her head again, this time more forcefully. "No, nothing like that. Layla asked me the same thing Saturday morning when I found those flyers, but I can't imagine who might do something like this."

Caleb pulled his cell phone from his pocket. "I'll get some of the boys over here to fingerprint the area around the broken window in the bathroom. Maybe they can lift some prints that will let us know who's responsible."

"I hope so," she said. He turned his back to make the call and then when he had finished turned back around to face her. She looked small, and tears brimmed in her eyes.

He wanted to reach out to her, to take her in his arms and soothe the tears away, but he knew better. He knew he was the last man she'd want to hold her for any reason.

She wrapped her arms around her middle once

again, as if trying to warm an insidious chill. "I know it sounds crazy, but I have this awful feeling that this is just the beginning."

"The beginning of what?" he asked.

"Something terrible," she replied, her voice a mere whisper.

Chapter 2

It was just after nine when the deputies Caleb had called in finished up what little they had been able to do. There had been no fingerprints around the window, although they'd found a black thread stuck on one of the shards of glass, a thread they assumed was from whatever the intruder had been wearing when he'd broken in.

Portia knew there was no way they'd be able to figure out who had smashed the window and crawled inside by a single thread of cotton.

As Caleb walked with the other men out of the day care, she looked around the room and wanted to weep. She'd worked so hard to make this a place of fun and love for the little ones who were in her care, and now it was all nothing but a big mess.

Melody had all the kids outside in the play area, but she needed to get them inside before the sun grew too hot and at the moment this was no place to bring children.

Caleb came back inside. "You have a broom?" he asked.

She looked at him in surprise. "Cleaning up a crime scene isn't your job."

He shrugged. "You've got a yard full of kids out there who are going to need to get inside pretty soon. Two sets of hands will make the cleanup go more quickly."

"They aren't coming back in here," Portia exclaimed. "I'll make arrangements for Melody to have them at her house until we figure out what's going on."

"You still need this mess cleaned up, now where's the broom?"

As he began to sweep the floor Portia went outside to speak to Melody. All the children had arrived for the day and she gave Melody the keys to the minibus they used for field trips to transport the children to Melody's house.

Melody assured her the children would be fine at her place for however long it was necessary and Portia knew she could trust her assistant with all the details.

By the time she returned to the garage, Caleb had finished sweeping up the floor. "You sure you can't think of anyone who's mad at you?" Caleb asked as he stopped pushing the broom and leaned on the handle.

She frowned and bent down to pick up the picture books that had been thrown off the toddler-size bookshelf. "I spent all day yesterday trying to figure out who might have hung those flyers, who might have such a big problem with me that they'd want to hurt me like that."

She straightened and looked at Caleb. She'd spent most of her time since high school trying not to look at him, trying not to think about him, and most of the time she'd succeeded.

She'd finished college with a degree in early childhood development and had devoted herself to her business, but that didn't mean she hadn't had time to date.

"Joe Castle," she said.

Caleb frowned. "What about him?"

"He's the only one I can think of who might have an issue with me."

"Why? What did you do to him?"

Portia felt the heat of a blush filling her cheeks. "It's not what I did to him, it's what I didn't do with him." She broke eye contact with Caleb to place the books on the shelf. "Joe and I have been seeing each other for the last month. You know, dinners out or an occasional movie, nothing serious. Last week at the end of one of our dates he tried to take things to the next level, but I told him I wasn't interested. I told him I thought it best if we didn't see each other anymore."

"How did he take it?"

She met his gaze once again. "He was irritated, told me if I didn't intend to get in a serious relationship then I shouldn't have wasted his time."

Caleb frowned, his expression inscrutable. "I've known Joe for a long time. I know he's got a hot temper, but this definitely doesn't feel like something he'd do."

"I know, that's why I hadn't mentioned him until now, but he's the only person I can think of who I've had any kind of issue with."

"I'll have a talk with him, see if he knows anything about this." Caleb swept the last of the plastic trash into a pile and then grabbed the dustpan.

They worked for another few minutes, putting some of the things back where they belonged and not speaking. Tension gripped her and she told herself it was because of Caleb, because this was the first time in years that they'd spent any time together.

The old saying was that you never forgot your first love and Portia knew it was true. She'd never completely been able to distance herself from the love they'd shared in high school.

Despite the fact that he'd broken her heart years

ago, she still remembered how it had felt to be held in his arms, how his mouth had plied hers with a heat she'd never known before or since.

"That's good," she finally said. "I'll call a carpenter and see about getting the bathroom window replaced and things will almost be back to normal."

"Except that you're afraid." Caleb stepped closer to her, so close she could see the golden flecks in his dark brown eyes, so close she could smell the dizzying, familiar scent of him.

His words gave the tense feeling inside her a name. Fear. She'd thought it was because she was close to Caleb, but since the moment she'd walked in here and seen the senseless destruction she'd been gripped by a simmering fear.

"This feels like such hatred," she said. "It's creepy to think that somebody could possess this much hatred directed toward me."

He reached out and touched her chin, a familiar gesture that might have ushered in a million memories if she allowed it. "Maybe you're taking this all too personally," he said softly.

A disbelieving laugh escaped her. "It's hard not to take this personally."

He dropped his hand back to his side. "It could be kids, some teenagers with too much time on their hands looking for a little excitement. If that's the case somebody will talk to somebody else and eventually I'll hear about it."

"I hope you're right," she said and for just a moment she wished he'd pull her into his arms and hold her, take away the chill that refused to go away.

And for just a minute she thought she saw in his eyes the desire to take her into his arms. It was there only a moment, a soft yearning that quickly disappeared and made her wonder if she'd only imagined it.

"I'll have a talk with Joe and see where he was last night and if he had anything to do with this," Caleb said, all business as he started to back toward the door. "And if you think of somebody else who might want to cause you trouble, call me."

"I will, and thank you for all your help in cleaning up," she said.

He nodded once and then walked out. As she watched him go she felt a small stab in her heart, a faint echo of the way she'd felt years ago when she'd watched him walk away that final time.

Crazy.

They'd had their chance at making it work and he'd blown it. He'd obviously moved on. She knew he'd been engaged a year ago to Laura Kincaid, a statuesque blonde who was two years younger than Portia and Caleb. The engagement had fallen apart and Portia had just assumed it had been Caleb who had called it off, who had probably cheated on her. After all, that was what he'd done to Portia—cheated on her and broken her heart and there was nothing to indicate to her that over the years he'd changed his ways.

Laura had left town soon after the broken engagement and Portia had heard through the grapevine that Caleb was once again playing the field.

Portia wasn't sure now if her rapid heartbeat was because she was still just a little bit afraid or if it was because Caleb Grayson still had the capacity to touch her in a way no other man ever had.

The rest of the day passed in a haze. For the first time in years the day care was silent on a weekday. No childish laughter, no sloppy kisses, just a silence that pressed in on her as she finished trying to clear up the last of the mess. The carpenter arrived late in the afternoon to put in a new window.

Maybe it would be best to keep the kids at Melody's for the next couple of days until they could figure out who was behind all this. She could take the time and give the walls a new coat of paint, she thought as she closed and locked the door.

She'd been wanting to put a fresh coat of paint on the walls for a while now, but had never found the time. There was no way she could have the children come back until she was certain there was no danger to them.

She hoped Caleb solved this issue quickly so she could get the day care back up and running, but in the meantime she'd use the time with the children absent to do some grunt work.

It was just after five when she went inside her house. She would sleep with one eye and her bedroom window open tonight to make sure she'd hear anyone who tried to break into the garage again. On second thought, she'd keep her windows closed and locked. Anything that was destroyed in the day care could be replaced, but she couldn't be.

The kitchen smelled faintly of fresh oranges and the chicken salad she'd made early that morning for the children's lunch. She tossed her keys on the table and then walked from the kitchen through the living room and into her bedroom.

What she wanted more than anything was a quick shower, her favorite robe and maybe a quart of chocolate ice cream for dinner. She positively didn't want to think about break-ins or vicious flyers—or Caleb Grayson.

Minutes later as she stood beneath the warm spray of water she found thoughts of Caleb creeping into her mind. She wondered who he was dating at the moment.

He'd promised to love her forever, had promised she was the only one he wanted in his life, and then she'd gone out of town for her grandfather's funeral and the rumors had begun, rumors of his betrayal.

She frowned and shut off the faucets, then reached for the fluffy towel that awaited her. Ancient pain, she thought. She wasn't that naive young woman anymore, and she'd learned her lesson well where Caleb was concerned.

Once she was dry she pulled on her short, green silk nightgown and a matching robe. It was not quite seven when she settled on the sofa in front of the television with a tray holding a plate of chicken salad and a tall glass of iced tea.

She'd just finished eating and carried the tray back into the kitchen when the doorbell rang. She went to the front door and peered out, surprised to see Caleb standing on the porch.

Maybe he had news, she thought as she cracked open the door. "Caleb," she said in greeting.

"Hi, Portia. Mind if I come in?"

She unfastened the chain and opened the door to allow him entry. As he walked into her living room, he looked around with interest.

She followed his gaze, wondering what he thought of her bright color scheme, the oversize throw pillows on the gleaming wooden floors and the bookshelf jammed full of books, knickknacks and pictures of kids who had passed through her care.

"Nice," he said as his gaze went first around the room, then slid down the length of her body, making her unsure what exactly he thought was nice. He sank down in the overstuffed chair next to the sofa.

Self-consciously she belted her robe more tightly around her waist and sat on the edge of the sofa.

"What's up? Please tell me you've solved the crime and the vandal is behind bars."

"Not even close," he replied with obvious reluctance. "I just wanted to let you know that I talked to Joe this afternoon. He insists he had nothing to do with the flyers or what happened here last night. I also talked to several high school kids to see if they knew anything about it, but nobody seemed to have any information."

"You didn't have to make a trip here for that. You could have called me," she replied. She wasn't at all sure she liked him being here in her personal space. She didn't want to smell his cologne when he was gone, didn't want a mental picture of him sprawled in her chair as if he belonged here.

"You were upset when I left here earlier. I wanted to stop by to make sure you were okay." His gaze was too warm as it lingered on her, on her throat, on her lips.

"You know me, Caleb, I always bounce back from things."

One of his dark eyebrows lifted slightly. "That's just the thing, Portia, I don't know you. We've been sharing this small town for a long time and we never talk."

She shrugged. "We say hello, we talk about the weather. There's never been a reason for us to have a real conversation before now."

"We definitely need to have more than a passing

conversation now. Joe told me that you were dating Eric Willowby before you dated him."

"Eric and I dated for a little while," she agreed. "But that was months ago. Surely you can't imagine that he'd have anything to do with this." She rose from the sofa, unwilling to share anything else personal with him. "I appreciate you coming by to check on me, but as you can see, I'm fine." She looked at the door, giving him the nonverbal message that she was finished with the conversation.

Caleb rose slowly from the chair, as if reluctant to leave. She walked with him to the front door and he turned back to face her.

"Are you sure you're okay? You still look upset," he said.

She was upset, but it had less to do with the break-in and more about how his presence affected her. "I'm fine," she replied, surprised to hear a slight tremor in her voice.

He reached up and touched a strand of her hair. "You are so beautiful," he murmured.

For a moment they simply looked at each other and Portia felt the past rising up between them. A mix of emotions cascaded through her. A snapping electricity combined with a heady rush of desire and mingled with a bittersweet pain.

His eyes darkened and softened and as he stepped closer to her she knew with a woman's instinct that he intended to kiss her.

Her brain told her to step back, to stop it from happening, but her feet remained frozen in place and as he leaned down to taste her lips, she raised her head to receive the kiss.

Hot and half-wild, that's how she remembered his kisses, and this one was no different. His lips were soft and yet commanding, but as he raised his arms to embrace her, she broke the kiss and took a step back from him, angry that he would try to kiss her, even angrier that she'd let him.

"That was stupid," she exclaimed.

He grinned, the boyish smile she'd once loved to see. "Maybe," he agreed. "But sometimes stupid tastes good. Good night, Portia."

As he stepped out on the porch she slammed her door and locked it behind him, angry that he could still make her want him after all these years.

She was right. It had been stupid to kiss her, but she'd looked so damned kissable in that sexy green robe that allowed the tops of her creamy breasts to peek out and displayed her gorgeous legs.

He got into his car and gripped the steering wheel with both hands to allow the wave of desire that gripped him to slowly ebb away.

When he felt more in control, he started his car and pulled out of her driveway. He'd spent much of his day not only trying to find out who had broken into her day care, but also asking questions about Portia, trying to get a feel for the woman she'd become.

Loving. Generous and *kind:* those were words that had been used again and again to describe her. So why hadn't she married and started a family of her own?

Yes, it had been foolish to kiss her, but he'd wanted to taste her mouth, see if she still had the capacity to stir him. The answer was a definitive yes.

But years ago he hadn't been enough for her. She hadn't trusted him, hadn't trusted in his love, and there was nothing to indicate that another round with Portia would have different results.

He wouldn't put his heart on the line with her again, but he definitely wouldn't mind laying her down in a bed of fresh, scented sheets and making love to her until they were both gasping and sated.

She'd allowed him the kiss, but he had a feeling there was no way she'd be agreeable to a night of wild, mindless sex.

She'd thought he'd cheated on her when she'd been out of town and then again when she'd left for college. She'd allowed rumors and innuendoes to crack them apart. It hadn't mattered that he'd proclaimed his innocence loud and long; ultimately she hadn't believed him.

He'd never quite been able to forgive her for that, and that betrayal from her, coupled with the killer blow that Laura had delivered to him, made him wary of attempting any serious relationship ever again.

As he entered his small house, the first thing he thought about was how gray and dismal his surroundings appeared compared to the rich, bold colors of Portia's living room.

Her living room had been filled with life, as if a burst of laughter was ready to resound within the walls. He threw his keys on the coffee table and sank down on the gray sofa.

Gray. That was how he'd felt lately, as if he were just going through the motions of life without any real emotion or joy.

Over the last month he'd watched his oldest brother Tom find love with a beautiful woman and her infant daughter, and Caleb had been surprised by the yearning his brother's happiness had pulled forth in him.

With a grunt of dissatisfaction, he pulled himself off the sofa and went into the kitchen to grab a beer from the fridge.

He popped the tab and took a long swallow as he eased down into a chair at the kitchen table. As always when he had a quiet moment to himself, thoughts of his sister jumped into his mind.

"Brittany, where are you?" he muttered aloud.

He knew with gut instinct that she was in trouble, although he refused to believe she might be dead. A missing persons report had gone out to all the news outlets in a four-state area and the brothers had checked her house for any signs of foul play, but there had been none. They had conducted search parties for days that had yielded nothing. The worst part was not knowing what happened and not knowing where to begin to look for her.

With a sigh he took another sip of his beer. His cell phone rang and caller ID let him know it was his brother Benjamin. "Hey, bro, what's up?"

"Tom wants us to meet him at the Miller place as soon as possible," Benjamin said.

"The Miller place?" Caleb said in surprise. "Why?"

The Miller place was an abandoned farmhouse on the north edge of town. It had been a foreclosure that had been for sale for a couple of years.

"He said Layla was showing the place to some out-of-towner and called him a few minutes ago to tell him there's a vehicle parked in the old barn. That's all I know, but Tom wants us there."

"Be there in ten," Caleb said and clicked off.

Caleb set the beer on the table, grabbed his car keys and headed out. It wasn't unusual for the Grayson men to act as backup for each other when something came up that didn't sound right.

Tom was a cautious man, which was one of his strengths as sheriff. Caleb, on the other hand, had a tendency to be impatient. He knew it was a fault of his, one that he'd have to work on to become the kind of deputy he wanted to be.

Even though it was almost eight in the evening when he pulled down the dirt lane that led to the Miller place, the sun was still warm and bright, although lowering in the western sky.

Tom's car was already parked in front of the house, along with a car he recognized as belonging to Layla West, Black Rock's most aggressive real-estate agent and Portia's best friend since high school.

"What's going on?" Caleb asked as he approached where the two of them stood in the front yard.

"Layla was just about to tell me," Tom said.

"I had an out-of-town client, and I brought him here on Saturday to look at the house. Today he wanted to come back and check out all the outbuildings." Layla pointed to the barn in the distance. "We went into the barn and in the back of it, underneath some blankets, is a car."

"What kind of a car?" Caleb asked.

"I'm not sure. It freaked me out and I got my client out of the barn and called Tom." She looked at Caleb's brother. "Nobody should be parked in there, Tom. This property belongs to the bank and it definitely wasn't there when I showed this place a couple of months ago."

At that moment Benjamin pulled up and Tom quickly filled him in on what had occurred. "You go on home, Layla," he said. "We'll let you know what's going on when we know something."

It was obvious she would have preferred to linger and find out the scoop. "Come on, Layla, I'll walk you to your car," Caleb said. Tom shot him a grateful smile.

"Portia told me about the break-in," she said as they walked across the tall grass. "Are you going to find out who did it?"

"I'm doing my best," Caleb replied.

"You need to do better than your best," Layla said with a touch of censure.

Caleb opened the driver's side door of her car. "We'll figure out who's bothering Portia, but in the meantime we need to figure out what's going on here."

"Be sure and let me know," she said as she slid into the driver's seat. "And be nice to Portia," she added as she started the engine with a roar.

Caleb didn't wait to watch her drive away, but rather turned and hurried back to Tom and Benjamin. "Shall we check it out?"

Tom nodded and the three brothers walked side by side to the barn. "I haven't received any reports of stolen vehicles," Tom said as he pulled open the doors.

"Maybe somebody just didn't want to pay to have it hauled away," Benjamin said.

"Or it's being hidden from creditors," Caleb added. "Nobody likes the repo man."

They found the car in the very back of the barn, and just as Layla had said, it was covered with old blankets. Only the grill was showing and the sight of it sent a chill through Caleb.

As Tom and Benjamin yanked the blankets off, the chill deepened. Brittany's car. For a moment none of them said a word.

It was Benjamin who broke the silence. "I'll go get some gloves," he said and hurried out of the barn.

Caleb peered into the driver's window, careful not to touch the side of the car. "Her keys are in the ignition, but I don't see her purse anywhere."

Caleb felt sick and one look at Tom let him know his brother felt the same way. Tom's face was pale and his jaw clenched tightly.

There was no way to believe there wasn't foul play involved. Brittany wouldn't hide her car and just walk off with somebody.

Caleb's gaze lingered on the closed trunk and a rising fear thickened in the back of his throat. As Benjamin came back into the barn, half out of breath from running, he handed each of them a pair of latex gloves.

Caleb pulled his on and opened the driver's side door. Carefully he leaned in and pulled the keys from the ignition.

His feet felt as if they weighed a thousand pounds

apiece as he walked to the back of the car. Benjamin and Tom joined him there as he carefully put the key into the trunk lock.

For a moment it was as if the entire universe held its breath. He could smell the fear in the air. Caleb twisted the key and the trunk lid popped open.

He nearly fell to his knees in relief.

It was empty.

"I'll call the men," Tom said, his voice deeper than usual. "We need to process this car and see if we can find anything that will let us know what's happened to Brittany."

None of them spoke of the fact that it might be too late, that if the car had been hidden here right after Brittany disappeared, then it had been five weeks since anyone had seen their sister alive.

Chapter 3

At ten the next morning Portia was back in town to buy paint. She hadn't slept well. Every creak and groan of the house had put her on edge, but thankfully the night had passed without further incident.

It was Ed Chany in the hardware store that told her about Brittany's car being found at the Miller place. Her heart ached for what all the Graysons must be going through.

Portia knew what it was like to have somebody disappear from your life, to wonder where they had gone and if they were still alive. Her father had walked out on Portia and her mother when she'd been twelve and for years she'd wondered where he'd gone, what he was doing and if he were still alive.

She'd never tried to find him, had believed that if he had wanted a relationship with her, he would have contacted her.

She hoped there was a logical explanation for Brittany's disappearance, but the fact that they'd found her car hidden in a barn at the Miller place certainly didn't promise a happy ending.

She'd just loaded the cans of paint into the trunk of her car when she heard Caleb call her name. As he hurried toward her she couldn't help but notice the shine of the sun in his rich, dark brown hair, how he walked with a confident stride that was instantly appealing.

"Caleb, I heard about Brittany's car. I'm so sorry," she said when he stood just in front of her.

His eyes darkened and he nodded. "Thanks. We're doing what we can to find her, but so far all the leads go nowhere."

Portia fought the impulse to reach out and take his hand, to offer comfort to the man she'd once loved with all her heart and soul. "Hopefully she'll turn up safe and sound," she replied.

"We can only hope. Tom is still out at the Miller place conducting a search but he sent me back here to hold down the fort with Sam." An edge of frustration tinged his voice and she knew he'd rather be out actively involved in the search than on duty in town. "And speaking of Sam," he continued, "he thought he saw somebody this morning who might be behind the trouble you're having," he said.

"Who?" she asked curiously.

"Dale Stemple."

The name blew a cold wind through her. "Oh, my God, I hadn't even thought about him." She frowned. "But isn't he in prison?"

"After Sam told me he thought he'd seen him drive by I did some checking. He was released from prison two weeks ago."

"What about Rita? Where is she?" The sun overhead seemed less bright, less warming as Portia thought of the couple she'd turned in to Child Protective Services two years before.

"Who knows? The minute Dale was arrested she left the area. I imagine Rita has probably remarried. She didn't seem like the kind of woman who would be okay on her own."

Portia nodded and had a hard time summoning up a vision of Rita Stemple in her mind. The woman had been thin and mousy and had rarely been seen in town.

"I just wanted to give you a heads-up that he'd been released and might have come back into town to give you some grief. I'm going to try to find out where he is, but you need to keep an eye out, too."

"Thanks, Caleb. I can't believe he didn't even cross my mind. I guess because I just assumed he was still in jail. You'll let me know what you find out?"

"Of course."

"And I hope Tom and the others find out something about Brittany."

His eyes darkened with pain and his shoulders slumped forward. "Thanks. Me, too." He straightened and drew a deep breath and then glanced into her trunk. "Planning a little work, I see."

"I decided with the children at Melody's for the time being, it was a good time for me to do a little redecorating in the day care."

"So you'll be home all day?" he asked.

"Off and on. I'm planning on stopping by Melody's on my way home to see the kids, then I'll be home until this evening. Tuesdays I always have dinner with my mother. But, if you find out something and need to get hold of me, let me give you my cell phone number."

He wrote the number on a small notepad and then shut her trunk for her. "There's no reason to believe that you're in any imminent danger," he said. "No threats have been made on you and it's possible it wasn't Dale that Sam saw. Sam said he just got a quick glance at the driver. I just wanted you to know that I'm on top of it and you need to be aware."

"Thank you, Caleb. I appreciate it, especially with you having Brittany's disappearance on your plate."

He smiled, although the gesture didn't reach the brown depths of his eyes. "At the moment Tom is working Brittany's disappearance and I'm doing everything possible to fix your world. Besides, I'm afraid if I don't you'll sic Layla on me."

She laughed, and it felt good. "Layla is a good friend."

"She's like an attack pit bull when it comes to you," he replied. He jammed his hands into his pockets. "Anyway, I just wanted to let you know about Dale. I'll be in touch if I find out anything else."

"Thanks, Caleb."

She watched him walk back toward the sheriff's office and couldn't help but notice that he looked as good going as he had coming.

As she got into her car she told herself that the tingly feeling she got whenever he was near was nothing more than an old memory playing itself out in her mind.

Did anyone ever really forget their first real love? Their first sexual awakening? Did the memory of that person always evoke the kind of yearning, the kind of electric sizzle that Caleb still managed to pull from her?

They'd both moved on. She knew he dated often and so did she, although no man had ever been as important to her as Caleb had once been.

She dismissed thoughts of him as she pulled away from the curb and headed home. Instead her head filled with thoughts of the Stemples. Dale and Rita had had two children, a three-year-old little boy named Danny and a four-year-old little girl named Diane.

The two children had only been in Portia's care for two days when she saw the signs of abuse. There had been bruises on Diane's forearm in the distinctive pattern of fingers and when Danny had called for her help in the bathroom on the second day, Portia had seen that his bottom was not only marked with lines from a belt, but also scabbed over in several places.

She'd immediately called Child Protective Services and a woman had shown up at the day care and had taken the children into custody. Portia had never seen Dale or Rita again.

She'd heard through the grapevine that Dale had been arrested for threatening a social worker and for keeping illegal guns in his house. Rita had left town and Portia had put the whole incident out of her mind except for occasionally wondering what had happened to Danny and Diane.

There had been some speculation that Dale's parents might step in and request custody, but at the time Dale's mother had been battling cancer and so the children had disappeared into the foster care system.

After a visit to Melody's where she got enough hugs and kisses to last for the day, she drove home. She unloaded the paint into the day care and then went into the house for lunch. Her plan was to spend the afternoon moving everything into the center of the room to prepare for painting the next day.

She supposed she was probably overreacting to the break-in by moving the children to Melody's, but she'd rather err on the side of caution where their safety was concerned.

Besides, she'd been wanting to repaint the interior of the day care for months and this seemed like a perfect opportunity to get it done.

When she left her house to return to the day-care facility, she carried with her a knife from the kitchen drawer and her cell phone. She felt slightly foolish with the knife in her hand and wasn't even sure she could use it on anyone, even to protect herself. But she was reluctant to be there with no weapon at all while she worked.

At five o'clock she knocked off working and went inside to shower and change for dinner with her mother.

As usual, a faint edge of dread coursed through her as she thought of spending time with her mother.

Doris Perez was a bitter woman who had never gotten over her husband walking out on her and with each year that had passed, her bitterness had grown.

It was duty that drove Portia to the weekly dinners. Her mother had no friends, her health was failing and Portia was an only child. She loved her mother, but there were times she didn't like her very much.

At six she got into the car to head to her childhood home eight miles away. As she drove she thought of the brief kiss she'd shared with Caleb. It had stunned her to realize that after all these years there was still magic in his kiss. His lips had held an intoxicating warmth, a faint edge of hunger that had excited her.

Although she'd halted it before it had gotten too deep, too breathtaking, there had been a part of her that had wanted to pull him back into her house, take him to her bed and make love with him. But the rational part of her knew that would be inviting heartache back into her life.

As she turned down the tree-lined, narrow country road that would eventually lead to her mother's farmhouse, she couldn't help but admire the play of the evening sunshine through the trees.

It wouldn't be long and the leaves would begin to turn red and gold and fall to the ground. Portia loved autumn, but it was always in that time of the year when she thought of the babies she wanted— not babies who belonged to somebody else that she watched during the day, but rather babies that were from her heart, a twenty-four-hour part of her life. The fall always reminded her that another year was about to pass and she still wasn't pregnant.

"You have to find a husband before you can have babies," she said aloud. Although she knew some women chose to be single moms, that wasn't a choice she wanted to make.

As the daughter of divorced parents and as someone who hadn't had a relationship with her father since he'd walked out on them, she wanted her children to have something different, something more.

Her mother sat in a rocking chair on the front porch. The swing where Caleb and Portia had spent so many nights of their high school years had been taken down years ago.

As Portia pulled up in front of the house and parked, her mother stood. Doris Perez would be an attractive woman if bitterness hadn't etched frown lines into her face.

"Hi, Mom," Portia said as she got out of the car.

"About time you got here. I imagine the salad is soggy by now."

"I'm sure it will be fine. I told you I'd get here around six-thirty." Portia joined her mother on the porch and gave her a quick hug.

"Come on in and let's eat," Doris said. "When your father was here we always ate at five o'clock sharp. I'm not used to eating this late."

It was the same litany every time Portia had dinner with her mother. She swallowed a sigh as she followed Doris into the cheerless kitchen, where the table was already set.

As Portia slid into the chair where she'd sat every night for meals while growing up, Doris opened the oven door and took out a homemade chicken potpie.

"How's work?" Portia asked once they were both seated at the table and eating.

Doris scowled. "I never thought I'd have to work. If your father hadn't left I would be spending my days having lunch with friends and puttering around the house instead of selling cosmetics to snotty teenagers at the local five-and-dime."

"You only work four days a week. That still leaves you three days to putter around and have lunch with friends," Portia countered.

Doris didn't reply, but Portia knew the truth: her mother had chased off all her friends long ago with her negativity.

"Did you hear about them finding Brittany Grayson's car in the Miller barn?" Portia asked.

"I heard." Doris shook her head. "Terrible thing. You know that poor girl is probably dead."

Portia's heart constricted as she thought of Caleb grieving for his sister. "I hope not."

"Have you heard any more on the break-in at your place?"

"I spoke to Caleb this morning about it. He mentioned that Dale Stemple just got out of prison. Remember him? I turned him and his wife in for child abuse."

Doris nodded. "A nasty piece of work, that man was. I always thought he probably beat up on Rita, too. She acted like she was half-scared to move or talk whenever I saw her."

"Of course we have no idea if Dale is even back in town or not," Portia replied.

"I'm sure Caleb has other things on his mind with his sister's car being found," Doris replied with a knowing gaze. "But the way I remember it you were always on a back burner when it came to Caleb Grayson. He's just like your daddy. Loves the women."

"Mom, please, that was all a long time ago. Why don't we talk about something a little more pleasant?" Portia exclaimed. The last thing she wanted to do was rehash Caleb's betrayal of so long ago.

For the rest of the meal they talked about the kids in Portia's day care, local gossip and the winter months that weren't so very far away.

After eating, Portia helped her mother clear and wash the dishes. "You aren't leaving right away, are you?" Doris asked when the dishes were finished. "I thought I'd fix some coffee and you could maybe help me on my newest puzzle."

Although the last thing Portia wanted to do was spend another hour or so working on a jigsaw puzzle with her mother, she agreed. In truth, Portia felt sorry for her mother, who spent her evenings working puzzles and hating the man who had left her so long ago.

There had been no secrets in the Perez family. Doris had shared with her daughter at a very early age that her father, Pete, had not been faithful. There was a part of Portia that resented that her mother had made her party to adult issues when she should have been a carefree, happy child.

She remembered her father as a big, affable man with a booming laugh and big, strong arms. When she'd been young she hadn't understood why when he'd left her mother, he'd also left her. As an adult she suspected that her father had been unable to sustain a relationship with Portia because that would have meant he'd have had to deal with his ex-wife.

He'd paid child support every month until Portia turned eighteen, and to this day Portia wondered if she would ever see him again.

It was almost ten and dark outside when her mother walked her out on the porch to tell her goodbye. Portia hugged her mother and wished things could have been different for her, wished that Doris had found some sort of happiness in her life, but she'd clung to her bitterness like it was a warm familiar lover and had refused to let it go.

"I'll call you tomorrow night," Portia said as she headed to her car.

It was a beautiful night. The temperature had dropped to a pleasant level and as Portia started her car she rolled down the windows for the drive home.

The road she travelled between her mother's house and her own was a narrow two-lane stretch of highway that was rarely used and lined with thick-trunked old trees.

The night air drifted through the window and caressed her face. She turned the radio on and tuned it to her favorite oldies station.

Portia hadn't gone far when she noticed the headlights of another vehicle approaching quickly behind her. Irritation surged up inside her as the truck drew close and its brights shimmered in her rearview mirror.

"Jerk," she muttered and flipped the mirror up to diminish the blinding glare. "Dim your lights."

Before she had her hand firmly back on the steering wheel she felt a jarring bang. "Hey!" she cried as she realized she'd been hit from behind.

She started to brake, assuming that it had been an accident, but before she could she was hit again, this time with enough force to wrest the steering wheel out of her hands.

A single moment of panic soared through her as she realized her car was out of control and one of those beautiful, big oak trees was directly in front of her.

She heard the impact just before her head snapped forward and made contact with the steering wheel and darkness sprang up to grab her.

Caleb had just shucked his jeans to go to bed when his cell phone rang. It was the deputy on duty, Sam McCain. "What's up, Sam?" Caleb asked.

"I just got a call from Gus Swanson. He and his wife were driving down Old Pike Highway and found Portia Perez's car wrecked and her unconscious. They're near Doris's place and I've called for an ambulance, but thought you might want to know."

Sam had barely gotten the words out of his mouth before Caleb hung up. He grabbed his jeans and pulled them back on, his heart thundering with urgency.

He snatched his car keys and was on the road within seconds. *Unconscious:* that didn't sound good. What had happened? He knew that stretch of highway was narrow, but Portia had driven it enough times to know it like the back of her hand.

So, what had happened? How had she wrecked? And how badly was she hurt? He squeezed the steering wheel tightly and stepped on the gas, unable to get to the scene fast enough.

No matter what their past, Portia had never moved far out of his heart. Even the love he'd thought he'd had for Laura hadn't rivaled what he'd once felt for Portia.

As always, thoughts of Laura created a hot ball of anger in his chest. What she'd done to him was unforgivable and even though it had been a little over a year ago, the rage he felt toward her hadn't diminished.

But he couldn't think about that now. He had to get to Portia.

His heart nearly stopped as he rounded a curve and came upon the scene. The front end of Portia's red car was smashed against a tree trunk.

Gus Swanson and his wife, Martha, stood next to the car and Portia was prone on the ground next to them. A sigh of relief escaped Caleb as he saw Portia raise a hand to her head. At least she was conscious now.

He jumped out of his car and approached at the same time he heard the sound of a siren in the distance. Good, the ambulance would be here within moments.

The air bag had deployed and as Caleb assessed the damage to the front of her car he knew her seat belt and the air bag had probably saved her life.

"Caleb." Gus greeted him with obvious relief. "She's conscious now but she was unconscious when we found her. We didn't want to move her but were afraid to leave her in the car with all the hissing and smoke."

"Did you see what happened?" Caleb asked.

"No, it must have happened just before we got here," Gus replied.

As the sound of the ambulance siren grew louder, Caleb hurried toward the car. Martha nodded to him as he approached Portia.

Her forehead was red and sporting a big lump, her face was as pale as the moonlight overhead and her eyes were big and vaguely unfocused.

A band squeezed his chest as she once again reached a hand up and rubbed her forehead. "I'm fine," she said before he could say a word. "I just want to go home."

"You're going straight to the hospital," he replied, worried when she once again closed her eyes. "Portia, can you tell me what happened?"

Her eyes fluttered open once again and in the bright silver moonlight he saw the fear that darkened the hazel depths. "Somebody hit me from behind and I spun out of control."

At that moment two paramedics moved in to get her on a stretcher. Caleb stepped back to allow them to do their job.

When she was loaded up Caleb walked at her side to the open door of the ambulance. "I'll meet you at the hospital," he told her as they were about to load her into the vehicle.

"Caleb, someone hit me on purpose. It was a pickup truck and it rammed me not once, but twice. Definitely on purpose." With that, she was loaded in and Caleb watched the ambulance pull away.

Her words rang inside his head like a deafening bell. *On purpose.* Was it possible she was confused about what had happened?

He thanked Gus and Martha for their help and then grabbed a flashlight from the back of his car. He approached Portia's wrecked car once again and shone the light on the back bumper.

There was no question that it had been hit from behind. The back bumper was smashed in as well as a portion of the trunk. He leaned closer and noticed flecks of black paint on the bumper.

When he straightened, a chill waltzed up his spine. If what Portia had told him was true, and the physical evidence certainly supported her story, then he wasn't investigating a hit-and-run accident, he was investigating a case of attempted murder.

Chapter 4

Portia just wanted to go home. She'd been X-rayed and examined by the doctor and now sat alone on the examining room table waiting the doctor's return with the results.

Her head ached. Heck, her entire body felt as if it had been beaten by a gang of thugs with bats and she just wanted the comfort of her own bed.

The room was cool, Portia being clad only in the open-backed gown. But she didn't know if her chill was from the room temperature and her attire or thoughts of what had happened out on the road.

She heard footsteps approaching and breathed a sigh of relief. Good, maybe she was finally going to be released. The curtain swung open and Caleb came in.

"I thought you were the doctor here to release me," she said.

"He's looking at your X-rays now. You feel up to answering a few questions?" He stepped closer to her and his eyes radiated with a sympathy that made her suddenly feel like crying.

"Okay," she replied and wrapped her arms around her middle, seeking some warmth. Her chill intensified as she prepared herself to answer his questions.

"How are you feeling?"

"On a scale of one to ten, with ten being the worst I've ever felt in my life, I'm about a twelve," she replied. "I'm sore in places I didn't know I had muscles." *And scared,* she mentally added. As she thought of those moments on the dark, narrow highway when the truck had hit her, fear overwhelmed any soreness in her body.

"Before they loaded you in the ambulance, you said whoever hit you did it on purpose." His gaze was intense as it lingered on her.

"He did." The chill intensified. "It was a truck. I'm pretty sure it was a pickup. It tapped me in the rear end the first time but I managed to maintain control, then it hit me again harder and the wheel spun out of my hands." A sob crept up the back of her throat, but she swallowed hard against it.

She was surprised to realize that what she wanted more than anything at the moment was Caleb's strong, warm arms around her. But she had to remind herself that it had been years since she'd found comfort in his arms.

"Could you see the driver?"

"No, it was too dark and whoever it was had the brights on. There was a terrible glare. But it was definitely a dark-colored truck."

"Black," he replied. "There were black paint chips on your bumper."

"Gee, that should narrow things down," she said wryly. Half the men in Black Rock drove black pickup trucks. "Joe drives one," she said suddenly.

"I'll check it out. Whoever hit you will have damage on their vehicle. We'll alert all the body shops in the area and check every truck that fits the description."

At that moment Dr. Debar walked in. "Caleb," he said with a nod. "If you could excuse us, I need to talk to my patient."

"It's okay. I don't mind if he stays," Portia replied. She doubted that the doctor had any information about her condition that she'd hate for Caleb to hear.

"You've suffered a mild concussion. I'd like to keep you overnight for observation," Dr. Debar said.

"No, I don't want to stay. You said it was a mild concussion. I just want to go home," she replied.

"You shouldn't be alone," Dr. Debar said.

"I'll be fine," she said more firmly. "Please, I really just want to go home."

"You want me to call your mother?" Caleb asked.

"Are you offering to make things worse?" she retorted. He knew that her relationship with her mother was trying at best. The last person she wanted to deal with at the moment was her mother. "Really, I'm all right. I just want to go home and go to bed."

Dr. Debar shrugged and looked at Caleb. "I can't force her to stay." He looked back at Portia. "While you get dressed I'll get your release papers signed, but if you have any dizziness or nausea you need to come right back."

Portia nodded wearily and breathed a sigh of relief as they left her alone to get dressed. What was happening to her life? She could have died if she hadn't had her seat belt on, if the air bag hadn't deployed.

Had the Swansons saved her life by being there? Had the driver of the truck had intentions of stopping to see if she'd died in the crash? And when the driver had found her still alive, would he have ensured her death somehow?

This was a nightmare with a very real, but shadowy, boogeyman she couldn't imagine the identity of. All she knew was that for the first time in her entire life she was truly afraid.

A glance at the clock let her know it was almost

one. If it wasn't so late she would call Layla and invite her to stay with her, but she hated to bother her friend at this time of night.

Surely she'd be safe in her own house until morning. She had good locks and strong windows. Still, the idea of being alone for the rest of the night scared her more than she wanted to admit.

"Are you decent?" Caleb's voice called from behind the curtain.

"As decent as I get," she replied.

He swept the curtain aside. "You're all set to go. Dr. Debar said to contact him tomorrow if you feel like you need some pain meds and he'll call in a prescription."

"I don't need pain meds, I just need you to find out who's doing this to me," she exclaimed.

"I've already got Benjamin checking the system for anyone who has a black pickup registered in their name in the area." He took her by the arm. "In the meantime, I'll take you home."

"What happened to my car?" she asked as he led her down the hallway to the exit.

"I had it towed to Wally's. He'll keep it in the garage until we get samples of the paint chips off the bumper and it can be fixed." He tightened his fingers around her elbow. "You could have been killed."

"That thought has crossed my mind more than once in the last half hour," she said. Although she'd never really quite forgiven Caleb for breaking her heart years ago, she was grateful for the warmth of his hand on her, the nearness of his body as they stepped out of the building.

She was beyond exhausted and had yet to really process what had happened. The idea that somebody had intentionally tried to kill her was as alien as the spaceships old Walt Tolliver, the town kook, insisted landed in Black Rock on a regular basis.

Who could want to hurt her like that? What had she done to make somebody so angry with her? Question after question tumbled in her aching brain.

Caleb led her to the passenger's side of his patrol car and opened the door for her to ease inside. The minute he closed the door she was enveloped by the familiar scent of him, a scent that instantly reminded her of carnation corsages and hot kisses and a night of making love that she'd thought was the beginning of her future.

She leaned her head back and closed her eyes, weary beyond words as a headache banged in the center of her forehead.

"You okay?" he asked as he got in and started the engine.

She looked at him beneath half-closed eyelids. "Of course I'm not okay," she snapped irritably. "My head aches, my body hurts and somebody tried to kill me."

Everything felt wildly out of control and she didn't know how to cope, what to do to make herself regain some modicum of control.

He pulled away from the curb and was silent. "Sorry, I didn't mean to snap at you," she said apologetically.

He cast her one of his charming half smiles. "If anyone has a right to snap right now, I'd say it was you. You've had a rough night."

"It's not just tonight. It's a combination of the flyers and the break-in and now this. I just don't understand what's happening to my life right now."

"We're going to figure it out," he replied.

She leaned her head back and once again closed her eyes, comforted by the ringing confidence in his voice. Despite any personal reservations she might have about him, she knew he was a good lawman. All the Graysons were good at what they did.

Within minutes they were at her house and she breathed a sigh of relief.

"Thanks, Caleb, for everything," she said as she opened the door and got out of the car. "You'll stay in touch with me as far as how the investigation is going?"

"Absolutely," he agreed as he got out of the car. He hurried around to her side and grabbed her elbow to escort her to the front door.

With each moment that passed, the aches in her body grew more pronounced and she felt as if her feet each weighed a hundred pounds.

"How's your head?" he asked as they reached the front door and she dug into her purse for her key. She was grateful that he'd thought to grab her purse from the car before it had been towed away by Wally.

"I have a headache, but I'm not feeling dizzy or nauseated or anything like that." She pushed the door open and turned back to him. "I'll be fine now," she said.

"I know you'll be fine. Because I have no intention of leaving you alone for the rest of the night." He moved past her and into the house. "Come on, Portia, let me help you to bed."

Caleb saw the faint glint of fire that lit her eyes at his words and realized at that moment there was still something between them, something hot and crazy that the years hadn't managed to douse.

"That's not necessary," she protested, but it was a weak protest.

"You heard the doctor. You aren't supposed to be alone now. You don't want to call your mother and I'm here, so that's that."

She closed the door and locked it. "I have to admit, I was kind of dreading being alone tonight." She walked over to the sofa and sank down on the cushions. "I'm not quite ready to go to bed yet. My head is still spinning with everything that's happened."

She looked small and vulnerable and a surge of anger filled Caleb as he thought of the person responsible. He walked over and sat next to her, fighting the impulse to pull her into his arms and promise to spend the rest of his life keeping her safe.

"I contacted Dale Stemple's parents yesterday to see if they'd seen or heard from Dale since his release from prison. They insisted they haven't had any contact with their son since he went to prison. I asked around town and nobody else has seen him. It's possible Sam was mistaken."

"Which puts us back to square one—who can hate me enough to try to kill me?" She rubbed the center of her forehead and released a sigh that pierced through to his heart. "Maybe Sam wasn't mistaken and Dale is here in town but just hiding really well."

"Maybe, but, Portia, we aren't going to solve anything tonight. You've been through a pretty major trauma. What you need right now is rest."

She nodded and winced. "You're right. I'm going to bed. The guest room is made up and you can help yourself to whatever." She stood and sighed once again. "Hopefully this headache will be gone in the morning."

He stood, as well, wishing he had some words of comfort to offer her, some assurance that no more danger would come to her. But he refused to offer her false promises. "You can get into bed all right on your own?"

She offered him a faint smile. "I've been doing

it on my own for a long time," she replied and then headed down the hallway.

It was ridiculous how her words hinting that she'd always slept alone filled him with an unexpected pleasure. He knew she dated a lot, but apparently those dates hadn't led to any real intimacy.

Since Laura, Caleb had dated, as well, but he'd also avoided any intimacy with the women he casually dated. He didn't want to get close, knew that lovemaking could evolve into heart involvement and he simply didn't intend to ever go there again with any woman.

At the moment his lack of a personal relationship in his life was the last thing on his mind. He needed to find out who was after Portia and why. And the disappearance of Brittany continued to haunt his mind.

Knowing that nothing could be accomplished until morning, he checked the locks on the doors and windows, then headed down the hallway to the guest bedroom.

The room was as inviting as her living room with a bright red spread across the bed and throw pillows in yellow and sky-blue.

He grabbed a pillow from the bed, checked the hall closet and found a sheet and then went back into the living room. He'd bunk on the sofa and sleep with one eye open.

Even though he didn't really anticipate any more

trouble for the rest of the night, he'd err on the side of caution.

It took him only minutes to make up the sofa, then take off his jeans and T-shirt and slide in beneath the sheet.

It was late and he was tired, but sleep refused to come as his head filled with thoughts of the woman in the next room. Were there secrets in her life she hadn't told him about, secrets that might hold a clue to what was happening to her now?

Black Rock was like any small town; the gossips loved to talk and everyone listened. He'd always assumed there were few secrets in Black Rock, but the truth was that nobody knew what went on behind closed doors or in somebody's mind.

He then realized that he'd always thought of Portia as his. She'd been his first love, his first lover and even though they'd only had a single night, prom night, together, it had indelibly written her name on his heart.

Even though it had been years since they'd been a couple, even though he had no hope that they would ever be a couple again, he wouldn't rest until the person who was tormenting her was behind bars.

He must have fallen asleep for he awoke with a start and immediately checked his watch. Just after six. Despite the shortness of his sleep, he felt rested and ready to face a new day.

He pulled on his jeans and then crept down the

hallway to Portia's bedroom. Her door was open and he peeked inside. She slept on her side facing him, her features soft and relaxed in slumber. Her hair was a spill of brown and copper against the pillow and the sheet had slipped down to expose the skimpy top of her emerald-green nightgown.

She looked beautiful and there was nothing he wanted to do more than crawl in next to her and kiss her awake. He'd love to stroke her silky skin until she was gasping with pleasure, but that would be the biggest mistake he could make. Instead he turned and headed back to the bathroom where he washed up and then went into the kitchen to make some coffee.

When the coffee had brewed he poured himself a cup and then stood at the window and frowned. The house backed up to a wooded area and there were trees on either side of the house, as well.

It had been easy for somebody to break into the day care without being seen. Her neighbors were far enough away that nobody would have heard the noise. It would be relatively easy for somebody to break into the house without being seen or heard, as well.

He needed to figure out what in the hell was going on, he thought as he sipped the coffee and watched the sun begin to peek over the horizon.

He was on his third cup of coffee and had made several phone calls when he heard the sound of water running and realized Portia was awake and taking a shower.

She was probably going to be sore, he thought as he checked the refrigerator and pulled out everything he needed to rustle up some bacon, eggs and toast.

Although he was eager to get out and start checking trucks and asking questions, his first order of business was to make sure she was okay.

The bacon had just finished frying when she made an appearance. "Over easy or broken yolks?" he asked. He tried not to notice how the lime-green T-shirt she wore clung to her breasts and transformed her hazel eyes to the color of lush grass. White shorts hugged her shapely behind and displayed her gorgeous long legs.

"Caleb, what are you doing?" she asked from the doorway.

"I'm making you breakfast. How are you feeling?"

She left the doorway and walked over to the cabinet to get herself a coffee cup. "Actually, better than I thought I would. My body is a little sore but at least my headache is gone. And over easy would be terrific."

"Sit," he commanded and pointed to the table. "This will be ready in just a few minutes."

She sat at the table. "I didn't know you could cook."

He crooked an eyebrow upward. "There's probably a lot of things about me you don't know. Just like there are probably a lot of things about you that I don't know."

She wrapped her slender fingers around her cup and looked at him. "Why do I get the feeling you're not just making small talk?"

He broke the eggs into the skillet and pressed the bread down into the toaster. "What are your plans for the day?" he asked, intentionally changing the subject. He'd just needed to remind himself that they had no real connection, that they'd been two different people when they'd been young and crazy in love.

"I'm thinking of doing something completely shallow and out of character and calling Layla to see if she wants to go shopping and have lunch."

"I think that sounds like just what the doctor ordered," he said, glad that she didn't intend to stay here all day alone.

The toast popped up and he flipped the eggs onto the awaiting plates, then he set the plates on the table and joined her there.

"What are your plans for the day?" she asked.

"This morning I'm going to coordinate with Benjamin and we're going to check out the black pickups in the area and look for front-end damage. This afternoon I plan on stopping in at Harley's Bar to see if Harley has seen or heard from Dale. If I remember right, the two men were friends before Dale went to prison."

"Maybe Harley is behind this," she said.

Caleb thought of Harley Danvers, the owner of a raucous bar on the edge of town. The big bald man was mostly muscles and tattoos and wore his badass attitude on his broad, ex-boxer features.

"I don't know," he finally replied. "Everyone knows that beneath Harley's gruff exterior is a big heart. I can't imagine him risking everything he's built here in town to do something like this for a friend, but I'll check it all out."

For a few moments they ate in silence. Caleb tried not to notice the play of the sun in her hair and the floral scent that emanated from her. He tried not to remember that single night of passion they'd shared so long ago.

He needed to solve this thing and fast. The more time he spent with Portia the more she stirred something inside him that was definitely unwelcome.

"After you eat I want you to make a list for me of anyone you've dated, anyone you've flirted with in the last year. I want to know anyone who was rude to you, anyone who made you feel uncomfortable even for a second."

"So you don't think it's Dale Stemple come back to get revenge on me?" she asked.

"I think the worst thing we can do is have tunnel vision and just assume it's Dale to the exclusion of anyone else." He ate the last bit of his toast and then got up and carried his plate to the sink.

"I don't see why we need to go back a whole year. Surely whoever is angry with me, if it isn't Dale Stemple, is mad about something that's happened recently," she replied.

"Not necessarily." He leaned with his back against the cabinet and gazed at her thoughtfully. "Emotions aren't always that clean and clear. Sometimes things simmer just beneath the surface for months, for years, and then they explode."

She held his gaze for a long moment and he realized he didn't know if he was talking about whoever was after Portia or his own unresolved feelings where she was concerned.

He shook his head as if to dispel such thoughts. "And another thing, I think it would be best if you stayed away from the day-care kids." Her eyes widened at his words. "Let's face it, Portia. I don't want any of the kids to become collateral damage and at the moment, it looks like somebody has targeted you."

Chapter 5

"He was surprised when I wrote down all the names of the men I'd dated in the last year," Portia said as she stabbed her fork into a piece of celery in her salad.

"We all know you're nothing but the town slut," Layla said with a teasing grin. "Besides, isn't that the pot calling the kettle black? Caleb hasn't exactly been a recluse. He dates a lot, too. He was even engaged for a while, although he managed to screw that up."

Portia looked around the café for the tenth time since they'd come in for lunch, wondering if one of the men at the counter, if somebody at one of the tables, had been the person who had run her off the road the night before.

She'd been targeted, that's what Caleb had said. But why? And by whom?

She returned her attention back to Layla and released a sigh. "It would be nice if all the dating I've done would have led to a Mr. Right, but I'm beginning to think there is no Mr. Right for me in this town."

"Tell me about it," Layla said dryly. "The only difference between you and me is that I *am* the town slut and I still can't find my Mr. Right."

Portia laughed and shook her head, as always half appalled and half delighted by Layla's outrageous sense of humor. Layla wasn't exactly promiscuous, but she'd definitely had more sexual experiences than Portia.

"I thought maybe after lunch we'd check out that new dress shop that opened down by the hardware store. I've been meaning to go in for the last week but haven't done it," Layla said.

"Surely you need to get back to work," Portia protested. "I don't want to take up your entire day."

"Seriously, do you realize how bad the real-estate market is here in Black Rock? I'm just lucky that I had a good inheritance from my parents, otherwise I'd be starving."

"Or buying fewer clothes," Portia said teasingly.

"Trust me, I'd rather stop eating than stop shopping," Layla replied with a grin.

An hour later the two were in Bernie's Boutique.

Bernice Clinton, aka Bernie, was a plump housewife who had decided to open the store in an effort to bring better fashion to the small town. She had an eye for what was hot and trendy and her store carried not just clothing but also shoes and handbags.

Layla was in heaven, sorting through the racks with a discerning eye and pulling out a half-dozen things to try on. Portia had no need for new clothes and was more than aware of the fact that until the children returned to the day care, her life would feel incomplete and no amount of shoes or purses could make it right.

When Layla disappeared into the changing room Portia sat on a tufted bench and visited with Bernie, but her mind was on Caleb.

Sometimes things simmer just beneath the surface for months, for years. His words played and replayed in her head. Had he been talking about the person who was after her or had he been talking about the two of them?

What could have possibly simmered in him about her through the years? He'd promised to love her forever, yet when she'd gone out of town he'd cheated on her.

Several of her friends hadn't been able to wait to tell her that he'd spent the evening at the café with Jayme Cordell, a lovely blonde who'd been two years younger than Portia and Caleb. Those same friends had told her that at the end of the evening the two had left together.

He'd proclaimed his innocence strongly and Portia had forgiven him. They'd resumed their relationship, but it had never been the same. She refused to make love with him again and he seemed okay with that, seemed to understand that she wanted to take things slowly.

She'd left for college and had only been gone a week when rumors began to circulate again about Caleb and Jayme and she didn't give him another chance.

Once a cheater, always a cheater, her mother would say. But her mother thought all men were cheaters and just needed the right opportunity to prove their vile natures.

Now, after all these years, Portia found herself wondering what had really happened between Caleb and Jayme. With the benefit of age and maturity, she recognized how twisted things could get when delivered from gossipers.

She also could admit that at eighteen years old her mother had been an enormous influence in her life and the memory of her cheating father had certainly played a role in her decision to kick Caleb to the curb.

She frowned. Why was she thinking about all this now? She couldn't go back and change the past and

Caleb was only in her life now as the deputy trying to solve a crime.

It was just after four when Layla dropped her off at her place. "You sure you're going to be okay here alone?" she asked, concern evident in her voice.

"I'll be fine," Portia replied. "Caleb said he'd check in with me later and besides, I'm not going to be chased out of my own home by some boogeyman," she added with a touch of false bravado.

"You go, girl!" Layla exclaimed. "You know, I could get you a gun if you think you need one. One of my old beaus has a revolver."

"No, thanks," Portia instantly exclaimed. "It would be just my luck that I'd shoot myself in the foot or somehow an intruder would get it away from me and use it on me. I'll be fine."

"Call me later," Layla said as Portia got out of the car.

Portia waved as Layla pulled out of the driveway. The two women had been best friends since fifth grade, their friendship challenged by their differences and nurtured by their sameness.

There had been no father in Portia's life and Layla's father had been a cold, critical man who had punched holes in Layla's soul with harsh words, a backhand and a lack of love. They were holes Layla tried to fill by jumping into bed and into relationships with men too quickly.

Portia started to head to her front door but paused

when a familiar car pulled in to her driveway. She smiled at the pretty blonde who got out.

"Hey, Peyton," she said to the woman who was dating Caleb's brother, Tom, and whose little girl was in Portia's day care.

"Hi, Portia. I heard about all the trouble you've been having and thought I'd stop by to see if there's anything I can do to help."

"Not that I can think of," Portia replied. "You want to come in?"

"No, thanks. I was just on my way to Melody's to pick up Lilly and thought I'd stop here for just a minute. I know Caleb is worried sick about all this. So is Tom."

"I feel a little guilty taking Caleb away from his search for Brittany," Portia said.

Peyton frowned. "Unfortunately there isn't much they can do about it right now. Tom told me that so far they haven't found anything in the car, no fingerprints, nothing that would tell them what might have happened. It's been terrible."

"Caleb didn't mention that to me."

"Caleb is the type who keeps things bottled up inside. I checked with Tom a little while ago and the search of the Miller property didn't turn up anything. Anyway, that's neither here nor there, I just wanted to check in on you." Peyton reached out and touched Portia's forearm. "I've been where you're at, Portia.

I know all about fear. If you ever need to talk, just give me a call."

It was no wonder that Tom Grayson had fallen in love with Peyton. She was not only beautiful, but she was warm and caring, as well.

"Thanks, Peyton, I appreciate it." The two women said their goodbyes and then Peyton got back in her car and Portia went into the house.

Peyton was right. She knew all about fear. It hadn't been so very long ago that her baby had been kidnapped and her life threatened by an unknown assailant. Tom had investigated the case and had not only managed to get baby Lilly safely back into Peyton's arms, but had also fallen in love with them both. The man behind the crimes had been Peyton's ex-boyfriend, who was also Lilly's father.

There had been rumors that a wedding was imminent between Black Rock's sheriff and the beautiful Peyton and everyone in town was happy that Tom had found the woman to complete his life.

The house was too silent and Portia found herself wandering from room to room, checking the locks on the windows, fighting the jangling nerves that threatened to take hold of her.

She'd told Layla the truth, that she refused to be chased away from her home. But, she had to consider that the person who had run her off the road probably also knew where she lived. She told herself she was safe behind locked doors and windows, with the promise of a patrol car in the area, but still she felt on edge, with a touch of fear simmering inside her.

It was just after six when Caleb called to check in. "How are you feeling?" he asked.

"Fine, tired," she replied, surprised by how the sound of his deep voice chased away a little bit of her fear. "Busy day?"

"Busy but unproductive," he replied, his frustration evident in his voice. "So far we haven't been able to locate the truck involved in the accident last night. I'm heading to Harley's Bar now to see if I can catch up with him. Are you okay there? I think maybe I should come by there when I'm finished at Harley's. I don't like the idea of you there by yourself."

Yes, a little voice screamed in the back of her head. *Yes, please come and stay with me.* But she refused to allow the words to leave her lips.

"No, that's not necessary. I'm fine. The doors and windows are locked, I'll sleep with my cell phone right next to the bed and there's no reason to believe anyone would try to break in here."

She couldn't let her fear rule her life, couldn't allow it to make decisions for her that she might later regret. She couldn't very well have Caleb move in with her for protection, nor did she want to.

His hesitation let her know he wasn't happy about her being alone. "I'll make sure a patrol car drives by periodically through the night," he finally said.

"That's fine. I'm sure I'll be okay," she replied.

It was long after they'd hung up, after she'd eaten dinner and gotten ready for bed, that she started to regret the fact that she'd told him she was fine.

She wasn't fine. The house that had always felt so warm and inviting now seemed alien. Each floor creak sent a wave of alarm through her. The sound of the air conditioner whooshing on nearly shot her up out of her chair.

At nine o'clock she finally decided to go to bed. She'd read until she got sleepy. She was in the middle of a good book and hopefully it would keep her mind off her fear and off Caleb.

She read until eleven, then, realizing sleep was the furthest thing from her mind, she decided to get up and fix herself a cup of hot tea.

As she went by the front door she peeked outside, and was surprised to see a car parked by the curb in front of her house.

Caleb.

What was he doing out there so late? The answer came with a swell of her heart. He was watching her house. He was protecting her.

Who was the man Caleb Grayson had become in the years since those high school days when she'd been so in love with him? And why, for the first time since those long, lost days, did more than a little bit of interest fill her?

What did he intend to do, park in front of her house for the entire night to ensure her safety? A warmth coupled with a sweet peace filled her. How easy it would be now to go back to bed and sleep, knowing Caleb was on duty.

And yet she knew it wasn't his duty to sit all night on front of her house. How on earth would he function tomorrow after spending the night in the cramped confines of his car?

You could make it easier on him, a little voice whispered. She hesitated only a moment and then unlocked the front door and stepped out on the porch.

In the shine from the nearby streetlight she saw his face and knew that he saw her. She raised a hand and motioned him toward the house, unsure if she was welcoming in her protector or the only man on the face of the earth who had the power to hurt her again.

He'd had a bad day. Caleb felt as if he'd been spinning his wheels all day long with no forward movement on Portia's case.

His talk with Harley at the bar had yielded no answers as to Dale Stemple's whereabouts. With no indication that the man was even in the small town, Caleb had once again focused on all the men who had been in Portia's life over the last year.

If that wasn't enough, thoughts of his sister had filled him with despair. When they'd found the car Caleb had hoped it would yield some clue as to her whereabouts, but that hadn't happened. He knew that there were missing persons cases that never got solved, but he didn't want his sister to be one of those statistics. Still, until something broke in the case, there wasn't much more they all could do.

He'd finally gone home, but had only been there a few minutes when he'd been filled with a nagging concern for Portia. He hadn't been able to quell the feeling of imminent danger.

He'd finally given up trying and had driven to her house with the intention of spending the night in his car. The minute her front door had opened he'd tensed, wondering if something was wrong.

She'd stepped out on her front porch in that sexy, little green nightgown and had stared at his car for a long moment. When she'd finally raised a hand to motion him to the house, it hadn't been alarm that had shot through him, but rather a stir of something very different.

He now got out of his car and headed toward where she stood on the porch, his heart thudding a rhythm that had nothing to do with duty or protection.

God, she looked hot with her thick hair tousled and the green gown barely skimming the middle of her thighs and exposing the swell of her breasts.

"Evening, Portia," he said as he reached where she stood.

"It's not evening, it's the middle of the night,"

she replied. "Did you plan on staying out there until morning?"

"That was the plan," he replied. He tried not to allow his gaze to slide down the length of her.

"Wouldn't you be more comfortable in my guest room or on my sofa?"

I'd be more comfortable in your bed. The thought jumped unbidden into his brain. "Definitely," he agreed.

"Are you expecting trouble?" Her hazel eyes appeared more green than brown as she gazed at him somberly.

"Not really." There was no way he could explain to her that faint thrum of anxiety about her safety that had been with him all evening. He had no facts, nothing concrete to go on except the gut instinct that rarely led him wrong. If the person who had hit her car had murder on his mind, then he hadn't been successful and Caleb didn't know if he might try again. "I just decided safe was better than sorry."

"I like the way you think," she said dryly and opened the door to allow him inside. She relocked the door behind him and motioned him to the kitchen. "I was just about to make myself a cup of hot tea before trying to go to sleep. You want something?"

"No, but I'll sit with you while you drink yours." He sat at the table and watched as she filled the teakettle and placed it on a stove burner to heat. It surprised him just a little that she didn't seem self-conscious about her night attire.

Once the kettle was on she joined him at the table. "Nothing new?"

He frowned, irritated that he couldn't tell her the case was solved and she had nothing more to fear. "Nothing. I talked to Harley and asked around town about Dale Stemple, but nobody has seen or heard from him. I also spoke to Joe Castle who says last week he lent his truck to his son, who lives in Oklahoma City."

She narrowed her eyes. "Sounds a bit suspicious, doesn't it?"

"I thought so. I have the authorities there checking it out. I should hear something by tomorrow. Walt Tolliver also owns a black pickup and I went to his place to check on it, but it was undamaged."

She smiled. "Walt is too busy seeing aliens to worry about trying to kill me. Besides, he and I have never exchanged a cross word."

He shrugged. "He's a bit out of it most of the time. I thought maybe he'd hit your car accidentally while prowling for his aliens, but it wasn't him. Oh, and I had a talk with Eric Willowby. You know he's still in love with you." He watched her expression closely, but at that moment the teakettle whistled and she jumped up from the table.

"Eric is a nice man," she said as she poured the hot water over the tea bag in her cup. After a moment she pulled her tea bag and added a dollop of milk and then returned to the table. "He'll make somebody a terrific husband."

"Then why didn't you keep dating him?" he asked.

She took a sip of her tea and eyed him over the rim of the cup. She released a small sigh as she lowered the cup back to the table. "Because he wasn't the one."

"The one?"

A whisper of impatience flashed in her eyes. "You know, the one I want to go to bed with each night. The one I want to wake up to each morning. He wasn't the one I wanted to tell my hopes and dreams to." She shrugged. "As nice as he is, as well as he treated me, he just wasn't the one."

"Maybe you're looking for somebody who doesn't exist."

"Then I'll just stay single because I don't intend to settle," she exclaimed. "Besides, why are you asking me these questions? You certainly aren't an example of marital bliss."

"At least I got closer than you have been," he replied and felt the burn of anger that thoughts of Laura always evoked.

"I didn't know we were in a contest." She took another sip of her tea.

"We're not," he replied easily. "I was just curious, that's all."

"What happened with you and Laura? I heard through the grapevine that the two of you had set a date for a wedding and the next thing I heard was that she'd left town."

He hadn't told anyone about what had transpired between him and Laura and he sure didn't intend to tell Portia now. "It just didn't work out." He forced a smile to his lips. "She just wasn't the one."

Portia stared down into her cup and then looked back at him. "Like I wasn't the one?"

He sat back in his chair, surprised that she'd bring up their past and equally surprised by the faint surge of resentment that filled him at her words.

Her cheeks flushed with color and she averted her gaze from his. "Sorry, I shouldn't have said that," she said. "The last thing I want to do is rehash the past. I have enough to worry about with the here and now."

"I agree, although there is a little bit of our past I wouldn't mind rehashing." His gaze slid down the length of her and he knew there would be no question in her mind about what he meant.

Why not let her know he still desired her? They weren't kids anymore, but rather two consenting adults who didn't need promises of forever to indulge in a little shared passion.

He leaned forward and breathed in her scent, that delicious burst of sweet floral and clean soap. "I think about prom night sometimes," he admitted.

Her eyes shimmered with an emotion he couldn't begin to identify. "Sometimes I think about it, too. But we were nothing but kids, Caleb, and what we shared that night was magical because it was our first time." She finished her tea and got up from the table and carried her cup to the sink. "There's no way to recapture that magic, Caleb," she said as she turned to face him.

He got up from the table, as well, and for a moment he forgot why he was here in her house in the middle of the night. He forgot that he'd come here to protect her from some unknown assailant.

All he could think about was how shiny her hair was in the artificial light overhead and how no other woman's kisses had ever stirred him the way hers had done. His head filled with the memories of the slide of his hands across her breasts, the throaty moans that had issued from her as she'd helped him with a condom on that night so long ago.

He'd had an older friend rent the motel room for them and for that single night it hadn't been a seedy, rented room, but rather a love nest for the two of them to explore the desire that raged out of control between them.

"Maybe we don't need the magic. I mean we aren't kids anymore," he said as he stepped closer to her. "Aren't you curious, Portia?" He took another step toward her, close enough now to see the flecks of gold in her eyes, feel her quickened breath on his face.

He reached out and swept a strand of her silky hair away from her face, then ran his index finger across her lower lip. Fire leaped into her eyes and emboldened him and he didn't give himself a chance to change his mind, didn't give her a chance to protest, but rather took her mouth with his in a searing kiss of hunger.

She stiffened against him, but didn't step back, didn't withdraw. As his tongue touched her upper lip and then slid into her mouth, the tenseness left her body and she seemed to melt against him.

He wrapped his arms around her, his heart crashing wildly in his chest as she entwined her arms around his neck. The kiss grew wilder, hotter, as it continued and she pressed her body against his.

Kissing her was the same…and yet different than it had been years ago. She felt sweetly familiar in his arms and yet it wasn't a boy's desire that swelled up inside him, but rather that of a man.

His hand slid up her back, reveling in the feel of the cool silk and the radiating heat of her body beneath. His mouth left hers and slid down the length of her neck as he remembered the sensitive spot just behind her ears.

Her breath caught as he kissed her there and then continued down the length of her throat. She tossed her head back in a familiar gesture from so long ago, and in that moment Caleb knew he'd been mistaken when he'd told himself he'd rarely thought about her over the years, that he'd stopped wanting her long ago.

She'd never moved completely out of his blood, out of his heart, and at the moment the resentment he'd felt toward her seemed distant and impossible to summon.

It wasn't until his hand slid around to cup her breast that she released a small gasp and jumped back from him. Her breasts rose and fell with rapid breaths and her eyes were dark and turbulent.

"Is this why you came here tonight? You've gone through all the other women in town and have now decided to start all over again?"

Any desire that Caleb felt was doused by the surge of old resentment that sprang alive inside him. He stepped back from her and shoved his hands in his pockets. "You never did understand the kind of man I was...I am."

"I'm sorry, Caleb. That was uncalled for," she said, obviously contrite. "I'm tired and it's late. Maybe it would be best if we just called it a night."

"You go to bed. I'll just bunk on the sofa for the rest of the night," he said.

She nodded and without another word she left the kitchen. Caleb watched her go, his emotions a curious battle between anger and want.

Had he come here tonight following a need to protect her, or a need for something else altogether? Curiosity, that's all it had been, he told himself as he left the kitchen. He'd just wondered if that crazy, hot magic they'd once shared would be there again with her.

And it had…for just a moment as he'd held her in his arms, tasted the sweet fire in her kiss, he'd felt that same yearning to be her everything, to be the one.

Her words to him had been an unwelcome dose of reality and reminded him that what they'd once shared had been broken ultimately by her inability to trust him, her inability to believe in him.

Apparently nothing had changed and he'd be a fool to attempt any kind of a relationship with her. He'd keep her safe. He'd do his duty as the deputy assigned to her case, but there was no way in hell he intended to let Portia or any other woman into his heart.

Chapter 6

Despite the lateness of the night before, Portia awoke at dawn with the taste of regret lingering in her mouth. Shame washed over her as she thought about what she'd said to Caleb.

Her words had been hateful and had nothing to do with the truth. Caleb wasn't a womanizer. Sure, he dated a lot, but why wouldn't he? He was handsome and single and, besides, he probably didn't date any more than she did.

She'd been wrong to say what she had, but she'd been desperate to create a chasm between them, had needed a defense against the incredible want that had built up inside her with his touch.

As he'd kissed her, as he'd held her so tight against

the lean heat of his body, all she'd wanted to do was take him into her bedroom and make love. The desire had been so intense it had frightened her and she'd had to do something to douse the fire.

She sighed and rolled over on her side to look out the window where the light of morning was just beginning to creep across the sky.

It was too early to get out of bed and so she remained beneath the fresh-scented sheet with only her thoughts as company. Maybe Caleb was right, maybe she'd never really understood what kind of man he was—what kind of man he'd become.

What if he'd always been telling the truth? What if he hadn't cheated on her with Jayme Cordell? She couldn't even remember now who had told her about Caleb's betrayal. She sighed once again. What difference did it all make now?

It had been ten years ago. There was no going back in time to change things. She'd once believed that Caleb was the one, but now she sensed a simmering anger in him that occasionally flashed in his eyes, that hardened the line of his jaw.

Maybe it was because his sister was missing, or perhaps it was some damage that Laura had left behind when she'd moved from town. Surely he couldn't have any residual resentment toward Portia for something that had happened years ago when they had both been kids.

Portia only knew that as much as she wanted Caleb

and he might want her, she didn't believe he was the one, didn't believe he wanted to be the one.

She frowned irritably. What was she thinking? She didn't want another chance with Caleb. She just wanted him to find out who was after her and to get her life back to normal.

She needed her kids back in the day care. She missed their happy faces, their smacking kisses and their hugs. They had been the most important people in her life and without them there was a huge hole in her heart.

She desperately wanted a child of her own, but for now she had to be content with her children on loan, and at the moment she didn't even have them. Caleb had been right, until they knew exactly what was happening it was best that she stay away from the children she loved.

Sick of her own thoughts, she got out of bed and headed for the adjoining bathroom, hoping a hot shower would banish all thoughts of Caleb and how close she'd come to making love to him the night before.

But as she stood beneath the hot spray of water all she could think about was how Caleb's kisses had thrilled her, how his touch had torched through her with a desire she hadn't felt for any other man.

She certainly hadn't remained celibate during the last ten years. There had been two men she'd dated with whom she'd been intimate, one who had eventually moved out of town for his business, the other eventually moving on with her blessing.

But neither of those men had affected her like Caleb did. He made her feel as if her skin was on fire and he was the only one who could put the flames out. She had to admit to herself that there was something strong between them, at least on a physical level.

By the time she was out of the shower and dressed she smelled the scent of coffee and knew Caleb was also up and about.

She owed him an apology and it was on the tip of her tongue as she found him in the kitchen standing before her window with a cup of coffee in hand.

He turned as he heard her, his expression guarded and distant. "Good morning."

"Good morning," she replied. "Caleb, I'm sorry about what I said last night, about you starting all over with the women in town."

A smile curved his lips but didn't reach the darkness of his eyes. "Don't worry about it. I've already forgotten it."

"It wasn't a nice thing to say and in any case that's not what I believe about you."

He shrugged. "It doesn't matter." He took a sip of his coffee. "Have you talked to Wally about your car?"

"Yesterday. He told me he hopes to have it back to me by the first of next week." She walked over to the coffeemaker and poured herself a cup of the fresh brew and then turned to face Caleb once again.

The deep frown that cut across his forehead did nothing to alleviate his attractiveness. His hair was mussed, that charming, errant lock falling down precariously close to his left eyebrow. She fought the desire to step forward and push it back into place.

"I don't like the idea of you being here all alone without a car. Maybe it would be best if I stay here on your sofa at night until we figure out what's going on," he said.

The idea of having him here with her at night both exhilarated and terrified her. There was no question that there was still an overwhelming passion between them and she feared allowing that passion to boil over. And she knew instinctively that if he stayed here at night, eventually it would explode.

"Actually, I was going to invite Layla to spend a couple of days here with me," she replied, although it hadn't been a thought in her head until that moment. "I'm hoping to get in a little girl time with her and convince her that it would be good for her soul to help me paint the interior of the day care."

"Why don't you go to her place and spend a couple of days there," he suggested.

"Can't. Mr. Whiskers and I don't get along."

Caleb raised a dark brow wryly. "I hope that's a cat and not the newest man in Layla's life."

She smiled. "A big, long-haired cat who for some

ungodly reason loves me. Unfortunately it only takes about ten minutes in her house for me to suffer a major allergy attack."

His features gave away nothing of his thoughts. "Whatever, I just don't feel right with you being here alone until we figure things out. Call and let me know if Layla can't come over."

"I will," she said. "You want breakfast?"

"No, I need to get out of here and head back to my place to shower and change for work." He drained his coffee cup and carried it to the sink.

It was early enough that he could have stayed for breakfast and still had plenty of time to go back to his place and get ready for the day. It was obvious he was eager to leave and she wondered if he hadn't really accepted her apology. Or maybe he was regretting his own lapse in judgment in the heated embrace and kisses they'd shared the night before.

He didn't say another word as she walked with him to the front door. When they reached the door he turned to face her. "I'm not going to lie to you, Portia. I want you." His eyes smoked with a hint of a flame. "Since the moment you came into the sheriff's office about those flyers, I've been thinking about making love to you again, dreaming about it when I go to sleep." He shoved his hands into his pockets, as if afraid of what they might do if not contained. "But make no mistakes, I'm not in the market for a meaningful relationship or any kind of relationship at all. Still, if you're interested in indulging in a little strictly physical pleasure, keep me in mind."

With that he turned and walked out of her house. She watched him go, her mouth slightly agape in shock at his words and the realization that beneath the shock was a renewed burn of want for him.

Caleb was in a foul mood and didn't know if it was because he couldn't figure out who had it in for Portia or because she'd gotten to him the night before, her sexy curves melting against him and her mouth hot and sweet beneath his.

And then there had been her cutting comment that she'd apologized for, but was an indication that she still had trust issues where men were concerned.

Portia called just after ten to let him know that Layla had agreed to stay with her for the next couple of days. His irritation rose higher as he realized he was slightly disappointed that her friend had stepped in to help.

Despite everything there was a part of him that wanted to be her hero, a part that wanted to guard her through the long, dark nights.

At noon he left the office and walked down to the café to grab lunch. The officials in Oklahoma City had called that morning to let him know that Joe Castle's black truck had no damage on it. Everywhere he turned was a dead end.

He and his brothers Tom and Benjamin felt the

same way about Brittany. No clues, no direction to look, and with each passing day a sinking feeling that they'd never know what happened to their sister.

At noon most of the tables and booths in the café were filled with people. Caleb took a stool at the counter and forced a smile as Linda Wyatt, one of the waitresses, came over to take his order.

"Tough day?" Linda asked.

"Does it show?"

She smiled. "You look tired, Caleb." She pulled her order form from her apron pocket. "Working too hard?"

"Maybe thinking too much," he replied. "Just give me a burger with extra pickles, fries and a glass of iced tea."

"No news on your sister?" she asked and then blew upward to move a wisp of gray hair that clung to her forehead.

He shook his head. "Nothing."

She gave him a look of sympathy and then left to place his order. A wave of depression swept over him. His sister was missing and things didn't look good. He couldn't even figure out who had nearly killed Portia in a car accident.

"Hey, Caleb." The deep voice pulled him from his thoughts as he nodded to Larry Norwood. Larry and his family had moved to Black Rock two months before and he was quickly gaining a good reputation as the town's vet.

"Larry. How's it going?"

Larry sat on the stool next to Caleb and offered him a friendly smile. "Good. Every day that passes, Black Rock feels more and more like home."

"It's a good place to live with good people," Caleb replied, a sense of pride for his hometown filling his chest.

As the two men ate their lunches they talked about the town, their work and the relentless heat that was forecast for the next several days.

It was a respite for Caleb to talk about ordinary, mundane things for a while, with the conflicted emotions that filled him when he thought about Portia and the fear that thoughts of Brittany always brought shoved to the back of his mind.

When he left the café, instead of heading back to the office he got into his car and pointed the nose toward the Grayson homestead on the edge of town.

It had been a couple of days since he'd checked in with his brother Jacob and he decided to take a few minutes and stop by the cabin where Jacob was staying.

Benjamin lived in the large house where they'd grown up and he made sure their brother had the supplies he needed. As Caleb drove through the entrance onto the Grayson property, signs of a working ranch were everywhere. Cattle roamed the pasture on the left and on the right a field of cornstalks waved in the hot breeze.

Benjamin enjoyed being a deputy, but his heart was in ranching. Caleb wouldn't be surprised if eventually his brother quit his law enforcement work to become a full-time rancher.

He drove by the house and onto a gravel road that led to a wooded area some distance away. As he entered the woods the cabin came into view when he was almost on top of it. He parked and got out, wondering for the hundredth time what had happened to Jacob that had him hiding out in a cabin cut off from the rest of the world.

He knocked twice and heard Jacob's deep voice tell him to come in. Jacob sat in a chair with a lamp on the end table turned on. Sunshine couldn't pierce through the thick canopy of trees that sheltered the cabin.

"Little brother," Jacob said and smiled, although the gesture didn't reach the darkness of his eyes. "What's going on?"

"Not much. I'm feeling frustrated and decided to take a few minutes and come out here to see you. How are you doing?" Caleb sat in the chair across from his brother. He knew better than to ask what was going on in Jacob's world, in his head, because he'd already asked a million times and Jacob refused to share anything with anyone.

Jacob raked a hand across his whiskered jaw and

leaned back in the chair. "I'm fine. Tom stopped by last night and told me there's nothing new on Brittany's disappearance."

"I'm trying to stay optimistic, but it's getting harder and harder with each day that passes," Caleb replied.

"So, tell me what else is going on in town."

For the next few minutes Caleb told his brother about the mayor's plans for a fall festival, Walt Tolliver's latest supposed encounter with aliens and Portia's problems.

"You two had quite a thing when you were younger," Jacob said. "I remember Mom and Dad worrying that the two of you would run off and get married before either of you had a chance to experience life."

Caleb emitted a dry laugh. "They worried for nothing."

"Portia hasn't married, has she?"

"No, she's still single."

Jacob gazed at Caleb with a directness Caleb had found daunting since he had been a small child. Jacob was the older brother who had always been able to get Caleb to confess to whatever mischief he'd made. One look from Jacob's dark gray eyes and Caleb had always crumbled like a cookie.

"So are there any sparks between the two of you?" he asked.

Caleb felt the scowl creep over his features. "Of

course not," he exclaimed. One of Jacob's dark brows rose and he smiled. "Okay, maybe a few," Caleb added. "But it's just a physical thing. Nothing is going to come of it. We got it wrong before and there's no reason to think that we'd get it right this time."

"You were nothing but a couple of kids before. Both of you have some years of experience and wisdom under your belts now." Jacob reached over and picked up the bottle of beer that had been sitting on the table next to him. "Want a beer?"

"No, thanks. I'm still on duty. In fact, I need to get out of here." Caleb stood.

"Let me know how those sparks work out," Jacob said with a wry grin.

Caleb walked to the door and then turned to face his brother. "Trust me, they won't work out. I'm a man meant to live alone."

A burst of laughter left Jacob, the sound rusty as if from lack of use. Caleb hadn't heard his brother laugh since he'd returned to Black Rock and for a moment he savored the sound. Then he straightened his shoulders and glared at his brother. "What's so damned funny?"

"The idea of you being alone the rest of your life. I've never known any man less inclined to choosing to be alone than you." Jacob's eyes darkened. "And trust me, I know all about being alone." Jacob raised the bottle of beer toward his lips. "Go on, get out of here. I'll talk to you later."

As Caleb opened the door Jacob took a deep drink of the beer and raised a hand in goodbye. Caleb frowned as he got back into his car.

Jacob had become another concern on his radar. He was drinking too much, spending far too much time alone, and it was rare that Caleb saw glimpses of the man he had been before whatever events had brought him back home.

Tom and Benjamin had jokingly mentioned that they needed to have an intervention for Jacob, force him out of the cabin and back into the world with love and concern. But Caleb knew that wasn't going to happen. All of them respected Jacob's need at the moment to stay reclusive. It was obvious he was working something out in his mind. Hopefully, eventually he'd rejoin the world or at least tell them what had happened to him.

As he headed back to town his thoughts skittered over the members of his family. Fear gripped his throat as he thought about Brittany and concern filled him when he considered Jacob. At least Tom had found love with Peyton, and Benjamin was just a laid-back, happy soul whose goal in life was to see everyone else just as happy.

The afternoon passed with more of the same, chasing down false leads and fighting against a frustration that threatened to be all consuming.

He left the office at dusk but before heading home he swung by Portia's place. He wanted to make sure that Layla was really there and that Portia wasn't all alone.

With each day that passed and in which nothing more happened, he wondered if maybe there was no further danger for Portia. Perhaps the crash on the road had truly been some sort of accident and the person responsible had simply been too scared to stop.

Whoever had a beef with Portia, maybe their anger had been vented with the posting of the flyers and the vandalism in the day care. Maybe he was looking for trouble where there was none.

Maybe he was inventing trouble in order to have a purpose in her life. The thought hit him square in the stomach and nearly stole his breath away.

Immediately he shoved it away. That was not what he was doing. There had been three incidents of violence directed at Portia. He'd be a fool and completely irresponsible not to expect a fourth.

He breathed a sigh of relief as he pulled up to the curb in front of her house and saw Layla's sports car in the driveway.

Good, at least Portia wouldn't be alone.

An old rush of feelings swept through him, a bittersweet pang of loss, of broken dreams and unrealized hopes. The familiar bitterness crawled up the back of his throat and he swallowed hard against it.

As the emotions swelled inside him, he knew his brother was wrong about him. No matter how many sparks there were between him and Portia, no matter how lonely he found his life, he was never going to give his heart to another woman.

Jacob was wrong. He was meant to be alone.

Chapter 7

"It's going to look awesome," Portia said as she stepped back from the bright yellow wall that they'd finished painting over the last couple of hours.

"To heck with the walls, what I want to know is what are you going to feed me for dinner? I'm starving," Layla exclaimed as she laid down her paint roller. "You've practically worked me to death this afternoon."

Portia laughed. "And just think, we get to do it all again tomorrow. We still have three walls left to paint." She threw an arm around Layla's shoulder. "And dinner is going to be pizza delivery. I'm too tired to cook."

Together the two women cleaned up their brushes

and rollers and left the garage and headed for the house. Once inside, Layla plopped onto the sofa while Portia grabbed the phone to order the pizza. When the pizza order had been placed Portia joined her friend on the sofa.

"I can't tell you how much I appreciate you taking some time off and hanging out here with me," Portia said.

Layla smiled and shoved a strand of her long blond hair behind one of her ears. "Work has been slow and I had vacation time coming, and I can't think of anyone I'd rather spend it with than you." She wrinkled her nose and frowned. "And I think it sucks, that I don't have some Prince Charming begging me to spend a couple of days with him."

"This town is definitely short of Prince Charmings," Portia agreed and her head immediately filled with a vision of Caleb.

He might have been her Prince Charming years ago but she'd believed his crown had tarnished and there was no way to get the shine back. All day long she'd wondered if she'd been wrong about him back then. Had it been her heart that had tarnished and not his princely crown?

She jumped up from the sofa. "Come on, let's go into the kitchen and get some sodas and get ready for our pizza." She didn't want to think about Caleb anymore. She didn't want to think about how much she'd wanted him the night before, how much that want still sizzled inside her.

Once they were in the kitchen Layla sat at the table and Portia pulled out plates and got their drinks. They talked about their work in the day care the next day, Layla's lack of real-estate sales and the fact that she might have to consider a new career path because of the current economic times.

"What would you like to do if you don't work in real estate?" Portia asked.

Layla paused a long moment. "I know it sounds totally out of character for me, but what I'd really like is to be somebody's wife, somebody's mother. I'd like a couple of years of being a stay-at-home wife and mother and building a home and then when the kids went to school I'd decide what I wanted to do with the rest of my life." She flashed Portia a grin. "Lame, huh?"

"Not lame at all," Portia replied with a new burst of warmth for her friend, "although maybe a little politically unpopular nowadays."

"I've never been one for following the politically correct path," Layla replied. "You know I had a giant crush on Jacob Grayson when I was young."

"Really?" Portia replied in surprise. "He was definitely nice looking but he always seemed kind of scary to me."

Layla grinned. "Your scary, my sexy."

"That should be the pizza," Portia said when the

doorbell rang. She hurried to the door and threw it open and gasped as she saw the tall blond man standing on her porch. "Joe!" she said in surprise as a tiny edge of fear sprang to life. "What are you doing here?"

Joe Castle was a handsome man with piercing blue eyes, blond hair and a tanned, weathered face. At the moment his eyes were cold and hard and his mouth was a thin slash of displeasure as he glared at her. "Do you have a problem with me?" he asked.

Portia held tight to the edge of the door, unsure what Joe might be capable of. "Of course not," she replied.

"Then why do I have Caleb Grayson on my ass?"

Portia breathed a small sigh of relief as Layla stepped up next to her. "Hi, Joe," Layla said. "What's going on?"

"I just want Portia to know that I had nothing to do with what's happening to her. I'd never hurt a woman and I'm definitely not into vandalism."

"Joe, I'm sorry if all this has made you uncomfortable, but Caleb has to investigate and the first thing he asked me was who had been in my life lately. I had to tell him we'd dated and unfortunately that put you on his potential-suspect list," Portia said. "I never even considered it might be you," she added. It was a fib, but one that instantly dispelled some of the tension in Joe.

"I'm glad to hear that," he replied gruffly. "We dated long enough that you should know what kind of man I am, and I'm not a woman abuser."

At that moment the pizza-delivery car pulled up to the curb and a young boy got out carrying a carton. "Looks like you're getting ready to eat. I just wanted to tell you to your face that I had nothing to do with all this." Joe didn't wait for a response but instead turned on his boot heels and strode back to his car.

Portia paid for the pizza and the two women returned to the kitchen. "You think he really came here to apologize?" Layla asked as she grabbed a slice of the gooey pizza and put it on her plate.

"Why else would he have come?" Portia asked.

Layla shrugged her slender shoulders. "Maybe for attack number four?"

"That's ridiculous. Surely he saw your car in the driveway and knew I wasn't here all alone."

"Maybe he thought the car in your driveway was a rental since yours is in the shop," Layla countered.

Portia took a bite of her pizza and frowned. Surely Joe didn't feel that kind of rage against her just because she'd decided they weren't right for each other.

The news is filled with stories of women being murdered because of unrequited love, a little voice whispered inside her head. "I just can't believe this is all happening," she finally said. "I keep thinking this is a nightmare and eventually I'm going to wake up."

"If it is a nightmare I don't appreciate you involving me in your bad dreams," Layla said, making Portia grin.

For the remainder of the meal the two indulged in a little gossip. They placed bets on when Tom Grayson and Peyton would get married, how long it might be before Walt Tolliver needed to be committed and Layla's penchant for bad boys.

"I think Benjamin Grayson is pretty hot," she said, "but he's just too nice for me."

Portia thought about Caleb's brother. Like all of the Grayson men, Benjamin was definitely a hunk but he was also the most easygoing and good-natured of all the brothers. Layla was right, she was far too tempestuous for a man like Benjamin. She'd eat him up and spit him out.

"Benjamin doesn't date much. If fact, I can't think of anyone he's dated," Portia said thoughtfully.

Layla tore a piece of crust in half and popped it into her mouth and chewed thoughtfully. "I can't think of anyone he's dated, either," she finally added. "I wonder what happened to Jacob? I haven't heard anything about him in years."

"Who knows? Maybe we are both meant to be old maids with lots of cats and only memories of our old boyfriends to keep us warm," Portia said.

"Mr. Whiskers is my baby, but he's no substitute for a man. Besides, I don't know about me, but I definitely know you're meant to get married and have a dozen babies. That's all you've ever wanted."

A faint depression settled over Portia's shoulders. Yes, that's exactly what she'd always wanted—and that's what Caleb had once promised her, love and family.

"Sometimes I wonder how different my life would have been if I hadn't broken up with Caleb when I was in college," she said.

Layla reached for another piece of pizza. "Maybe not so different, except that you'd be watching your own kids along with everyone else's."

"I sometimes wonder if I was wrong to listen to gossip instead of listening to Caleb."

"Possibly," Layla replied easily. "There were a lot of girls who were jealous of you in high school. Caleb was one of the hottest guys in the school and you had him wrapped around your little finger from your sophomore year on. Lots of girls would have loved to see the two of you break up so they could have a chance with him. But it's all water under the bridge now, right?"

"Right." Portia frowned thoughtfully. "But I have to confess that I have just a little bit of regret inside me."

"Regret is kind of a wasted emotion unless it brings some sort of lesson with it," Layla replied. "Of course it would be nice if we could go back and fix all the things we regret."

Portia thought of the hardness she'd seen in Caleb's eyes that morning. Was she partially responsible for that faint edge of anger she occasionally saw in the depths of his eyes?

She didn't know, but what she suspected was there was no way to fix what had gone wrong between them, no way to reclaim the magic that they had had before. Besides, he'd made it clear that he was only interested in having sex with her again, not in having a real, meaningful relationship.

They finished eating and moved into the living room for more girl talk. The phone rang at eight-thirty. It was Caleb checking in to make sure they were okay.

The sound of his deep voice caused a whisper of a shiver inside her, a shiver of the sweet desire she'd felt for him the night before. She assured him they were fine, that Layla was staying with her for the rest of the week and the call ended.

"I know I have a reputation as a party girl, but all that painting and moving furniture wore me slick," Layla said as she stifled a yawn with the back of her hand.

"I'm pooped, too," Portia admitted, although she thought her exhaustion came more from too many thoughts about Caleb than from the physical work she'd accomplished that day.

"You aren't going to get me up at the crack of dawn, are you?" Layla asked as the two headed down the hallway to the bedrooms. "You know how much I need my beauty sleep."

"I promise I won't wake you too early," Portia replied as she turned on the light in the guest bedroom. She gave Layla a grateful hug. "Thanks."

"For what?" Layla asked.

"For being here. For being my friend."

Layla grinned. "I have to be your friend, you know all my secrets."

Portia laughed and released her. "You know where everything is, but if you need something you can't find just let me know."

"I'll be fine," Layla assured her. The two said good night and Portia headed for her bedroom at the end of the hallway.

Like Layla, she was exhausted. Her arm muscles and back ached from the strain of wielding a paint roller, and a hot shower sounded like heaven at the moment.

Minutes later as she stood beneath the spray of hot water, she thought of the work they'd accomplished that day. The yellow paint had easily covered the drab beige that had been on the walls and when finished would give the area a cheerful atmosphere that the children would enjoy.

She'd called Melody that morning to check on how the children were doing at her house. Melody assured her everything was fine but the kids missed Ms. Portia.

While she couldn't put her life on hold forever, she explained to Melody that she just didn't want to take a chance being around the kids until this matter was resolved. She would die if one of the children got hurt or worse because some nut was after her.

When would she know if it was safe to have the children back where they belonged? When would she be safe to resume her normal day-to-day activities?

Maybe she and Caleb had overreacted to everything that had happened. Sure, it was obvious that somebody was mad at her, somebody didn't like her, but maybe that bump on her car had been the last gasp of somebody's ire.

Finished with her shower, she pulled on her nightgown and got into bed with only the lamp on her nightstand aglow. There was no other sound in the house so she knew Layla was also in bed.

Warmth filled her heart as she thought of her friend. When she'd called Layla and asked her to stay with her for a couple of days, Layla hadn't hesitated. Within an hour she'd arrived with a suitcase and a smile, ready to support Portia in whatever she needed.

Portia wished Layla would find a man who would love her to distraction, a man who could manage her volatile nature, who would see beyond her flaws and find the gold inside.

With a deep sigh Portia reached out and turned off her lamp. The room was plunged into darkness with just the faint cast of the moon spilling in through the window.

She thought that it would take her forever to fall asleep, but almost immediately she not only slept, but dreamed. And in her dream it was prom night and she was in the motel room with Caleb.

Her stomach was knotted with a delicious tension as she saw the rose petals on the bed, saw the desire that flamed hot and wild in Caleb's eyes. This was it—in the next few minutes she would give her virginity to the man she loved.

Although she was nervous, she wasn't afraid. She knew Caleb would be gentle, that he would take good care of the gift she was about to give to him. She knew this was the right thing to do, what she wanted to do more than anything else.

As he gathered her into his arms, her heart tap-danced a quick rhythm of desire. And when his mouth claimed hers, hot and greedy, she returned the kiss with fervor.

The kiss chased away any lingering doubt that might have entered her mind. He had her heart and now it was finally time to give him the whole of her body.

They fell to the bed where the scent of roses filled her head and his mouth found the spot behind her ear that always made her gasp with pleasure.

"I love you, Portia. I'll always love you," he whispered into her ear.

His words made her heart sing. "I love you, too. Forever and always," she replied.

"I promise you that there will never be another girl for me. I'll love you until the day I die." His voice trembled with emotion.

His arms wrapped around her and his fingers found the top of the zipper that ran down the length of the back of the royal-blue prom dress. The sound of the zipper hissing downward shot shivers of anticipation down her spine. However, as the sound continued on…and on…a niggle of anxiety weighed in her chest.

It shouldn't be taking so long to unzip the dress and yet that faint hissing sound continued. When it finally stopped she snapped awake and her heart thundered in her chest in a fight-or-flight response she didn't understand.

She lay for a long moment, eyes closed and every muscle in her body inexplicably tensed. What about the dream had created such an intense sense of unease? A sense of danger?

She cracked open her eyes and in an instant her mind took in two things. The first was the screen at the window that had been cut and hung askew. That was the sound she'd heard. The second thing she saw was the dark shadow that rushed at her.

Before she had a chance to scream the figure was on top of her with strong hands wrapped around her throat. Portia could tell that the hands were covered by latex gloves, the cool plastic chilling her to the bone.

She struggled, but found herself trapped by the sheet covering her. Frantic, she tried to escape the cotton cocoon but couldn't get loose.

The hands around Portia's neck squeezed tighter and fingers tore into her skin as panic screamed inside her. She thrashed her arms and legs in an effort to get free, to be able to fight back.

She couldn't tell anything about her attacker other than the fact that the face was covered with a ski mask and there was almost inhuman strength in the hands at her throat. She saw the glitter of eyes, but couldn't discern the color in the darkness of the room.

The attacker didn't say a word but emitted raspy, rapid breathing as those hands continued to strangle Portia. She wished for a voice, something she could hear that would identify the person.

Tears blinded her as she realized if she didn't do something she was going to die right here in her bedroom with Layla only a room and a scream away.

She couldn't breathe and a new darkness was closing in all around her as the fingers pressed tighter and tighter into her throat. Tiny stars exploded in her head as her brain begged for oxygen.

Finally she managed to get an arm free from the sheet and she swung it hard at the side of the head of the attacker. The hands around Portia's throat slipped slightly and she drew in a deep breath as she struck once again with her fist.

She tried to summon a scream, but nothing came out. Again and again she slammed her fist against the attacker's face and shoulders and then she managed to get a leg out from beneath the sheet and began to kick, as well.

The intruder drove a fist into Portia's jaw, snapping her head back against the pillow and finally, a scream ripped from her throat.

"Portia!" Layla's voice sounded from the distance. "Portia, are you all right? I'm coming in there and I've got my gun."

In the flash of an eyeblink the attacker was up and off the bed and back through the torn window screen to the outside.

Portia gulped in deep breaths of air and sat up at the same time her bedroom door flew open and the overhead light went on.

If she hadn't been so terrified, she might have laughed at the sight of Layla in a hot-pink camisole and matching bikini bottoms and wielding not a gun, but a hair flatiron in her hands.

She was crouched as if ready to spring and looked like a high-fashion ninja warrior. But instead of laughing, Portia grabbed her burning throat and hoarsely cried out to her friend.

Layla threw down the hair iron and ran to the

window and closed and locked it, then rushed to Portia's side. "Are you okay? Oh, God, Portia. Who was here? Did you get a look at who it was?"

Portia shook her head as she rubbed her aching neck and then moved her hand to touch her jaw. Cold. She was so cold.

It had only been a couple of hours ago that she'd wondered if she and Caleb had been overreacting to the events of the last couple of days.

Caleb.

She had to call him. She needed to tell him what had happened. A sob wrenched up her aching throat as Layla helped her out of the bed, but she swallowed it as she desperately tried to stay in control.

She needed to get out of this room, away from the window. She was afraid the person might come back to finish the job, afraid that this nightmare would never be over.

Layla seemed to sense her need and led her to the bedroom door. She didn't say anything but held tight as if aware of how close she'd come to losing her friend.

If Portia hadn't managed to release that scream, there was no doubt in her mind that Layla would have found her dead in her bed in the morning. She leaned weakly against Layla, her body trembling violently as she played and replayed the last few minutes in her mind.

Those hands had been so strong and so intent on

squeezing the life from her and they'd come so close to success.

When they were in the living room Portia grabbed the phone and quickly dialed Caleb's cell phone number. Layla sat next to her on the sofa, her face pale with shock and worry.

Portia held it together until she heard the sound of his deep, sleepy voice.

"Caleb," she said. "I need you." The control she'd tried so hard to maintain snapped and she began to weep.

Chapter 8

Caleb had never driven so fast down the streets of Black Rock. Thankfully at two-thirty in the morning there were no other cars on the road to get in his way.

The phone call from Portia had scared the hell out of him. All he'd managed to get out of her was that she needed him before Layla had gotten on the phone and told him somebody had come through the bedroom window and had tried to strangle Portia.

He gripped the steering wheel tightly as he made a right turn down the street that would take him to Portia's place.

Dammit, whoever had broken in her house had balls of steel. They had to have seen Layla's car in the driveway and that still hadn't deterred them from trying to get to Portia.

He'd called Tom and Benjamin and asked them to meet him at Portia's. It was a crime scene and he couldn't take care of the situation on his own.

When he pulled up to Portia's every light in the house shone and he jumped out of his car and hurried to the door. "Portia, it's me," he said as he banged on the door. Layla let him inside and he strode into the living room. Portia was up and off the sofa and into his arms in an instant.

She trembled violently and cried into the front of his shirt. He tightened his embrace and looked at Layla, who sat on the sofa. She wore a short pink robe and a look of horror. Portia wore her robe, too, the silk material cool against him.

"He came in through the bedroom window," Layla said. "He cut the screen and got the window open and came inside and he tried to strangle her." Layla's voice rose an octave. "He tried to kill her, Caleb. If I hadn't been here I don't know what would have happened."

"You're sure it was a man?" he asked as Portia's sobs began to subside.

She finally moved from his embrace and looked up at him, her eyes filled with turbulent emotions. He saw the redness of her jaw and throat and wanted to hit somebody, wanted to smash the perpetrator in the face.

"I don't know. All I can tell you is that whoever it was, was strong." She raised a hand and touched her neck. "He wore a ski mask and it was so dark I couldn't tell anything about him." She moved to sit on the sofa and at that moment Tom and Benjamin arrived.

For the next hour the men processed the window and the bedroom, questioned Portia and Layla over and over again and tried to find something that might lead them to the identity of the intruder.

An ambulance arrived and the paramedics checked out Portia, looking at her throat and jaw and making the assessment that she didn't need emergency care, and at Portia's insistence had finally left.

Unfortunately, everything had happened so fast, she hadn't gotten a really good impression of the person who'd attacked her. She wasn't sure about height or weight and couldn't tell them hair or eye color.

Throughout this time all Caleb could think about was how close she'd come to being killed. His heart beat an unnatural rhythm throughout the questioning, a combination of fear for her and suppressed rage.

If he looked at her red jaw and bruised throat for too long he feared losing himself in that rage. He knew if that happened he wouldn't be able to do his job properly.

It was after four when Tom and Benjamin were finished. They'd collected her bedding to be checked for any trace evidence. The window had yielded no fingerprints, but they hadn't expected to find any since Portia was certain the person had worn gloves.

"You're coming home with me," he said to Portia as Tom and Benjamin went out the front door.

She hesitated and it was Layla who took her by the hands. "Go, Portia. Go home with Caleb and let him keep you safe for the rest of the night. I love you dearly, but I can't keep you safe like he will."

"I'll just get some things together." She got off the sofa but hesitated.

"I'll go with you," Caleb said, easily guessing that she didn't want to go into the bedroom alone. She gave him a grateful smile. "Layla, just hang tight and we'll follow you home," he said as he headed down the hallway with Portia.

He stood in the doorway as she pulled a small suitcase from her closet and began to gather some clothes. They didn't speak. He had a feeling that at least for the moment she was all talked out.

Again a wealth of anger filled him as he glanced at the window and the bare mattress. "When I find him, I'll kill him." The words fell from his mouth before he realized he was speaking out loud.

"No, you won't," she replied. "You'll arrest him and do it the right way because that's the kind of honorable man you are." She went into the adjoining bathroom and he stared after her, surprised and touched by her assessment of him.

She returned a moment later carrying a makeup bag, hairbrush and a bottle of shampoo. She added those to her clothes and then shut the suitcase. "I'm ready. Let's get out of here."

When they returned to the living room Layla had changed into street clothes, had her bags ready to go, and they all left the house. As Caleb and Portia got into his car and Layla got into hers, Caleb looked around the neighborhood, hoping that nobody was watching them, yet wishing he'd see the perp hiding in the shadows so he could chase him down and smash his face in as payback for the bruised jaw and neck on Portia.

"I underestimated the person who is after you," he said once they were on the road behind Layla's car. "I assumed having somebody with you, anybody with you, would keep you safe." He slammed a hand against the dashboard. "Dammit, I can't believe he tried to get to you with Layla in the next room."

"If I hadn't awakened when I did, he would have succeeded. He would have been on top of me and strangled me to death before I could make a sound." She wrapped her arms around her middle, as if possessed by a deep chill. "Thank God I managed to scream. And when Layla yelled that she was coming, that she had a gun, that sent him back out the window."

They pulled up in front of Layla's house and she got out of her car and walked back to passenger side of his vehicle. Portia lowered her window.

"I would have flat-ironed his ass," Layla said and Caleb was grateful for the sharp burst of laughter that left Portia's lips. It lasted only a second, but it let him know she was going to be all right. He admired the strength she possessed in not falling into hysterics about what she'd endured.

"Thanks, Layla," she said. "I can't tell you how much I appreciate you. You saved my life tonight."

Layla flashed Portia a bright smile. "When this is all over buy me lunch and we'll call it even."

"Done," Portia replied.

Caleb remained in the driveway until Layla was safely inside her house and then he pulled out and headed toward his place.

The drive to his house was silent. Portia leaned her head back and closed her eyes and Caleb tried desperately not to look at the marks around her throat.

She was wrong about one thing. If he'd been in that bedroom when the person had been throttling her, Caleb would have killed him. There would have been no arrest, no judge and jury, just justice done with a vengeance.

The attacker had been stupid to try to get to her tonight when she hadn't been alone. Maybe he'd thought he was big enough, strong enough to take them both out. Whatever the case, it spoke of a hatred so intense the potential killer was willing to take big chances.

As he pulled into his driveway and turned off the engine, Portia opened her eyes and sat up. "What happens now?" she asked, her voice holding a weariness he'd never heard before.

"Right now we get some sleep and then we figure things out in the morning," he said. He got out of the car and she did, as well, her gaze furtive as she looked around the immediate area.

Caleb grabbed her suitcase from the backseat and then took her by the elbow and led her to the front door. "You'll be safe here, Portia," he said, not a hint of doubt in his voice. There was no way in hell he'd allow anyone to get to her while she was under his roof.

She raised a hand to her throat and nodded as he unlocked the door and ushered her into the living room. "Do you need some ice to put on that?" he asked as he dropped her bag to the floor.

"No, it will be okay," she replied and lowered her hand to her side.

"What about your jaw? It looks like it's going to bruise, too."

"It's all right. I just need to get some sleep. I'm sure things will look brighter in the morning." She tried to smile but tears filled her eyes. "Won't they look brighter in the morning, Caleb?"

Although he absolutely refused to fall in love with her again, there was no way he could see the need, the fear in her and not respond.

He pulled her toward him and she burrowed into him, pressing her trembling body tight against his. He knew the emotion that drove her into his arms was nothing more than fear and the residual horror of what she'd just been through, but that didn't stop him from responding to her nearness.

As he stroked his hand down her back in an effort to soothe her, his head filled with the dizzying scent of her hair, and the warmth of her sweet curves lit a tiny fire in the pit of his stomach.

He held her for only a moment, then stepped back, afraid she might feel his arousal. "Let's get you settled in," he said. He picked up her suitcase from the floor and carried it down the hallway to the guest room.

"It's not much," he said as he set the suitcase on the bed. He followed her gaze as it tracked around the room. There wasn't much to see. A single-size bed was against one wall covered in a drab, brown bedspread. A dresser stood against another wall, the top holding only a small vase with plastic yellow daisies.

"It's fine," she said.

"The bathroom is right across the hall," he said.

"I'll be right back." She left the room and went into the bathroom. While she was gone Caleb pulled off the bedspread and turned down the sheet. What he wanted to do was lay her down and make love to her until that fear in her eyes was replaced with passion. But he knew that wasn't what she needed. By the time he finished with the bed she came back into the room.

"Thank you, Caleb, for bringing me here. There was no way I could go back to sleep in my room, in my house." She wrapped her arms around her waist and looked at him with those beautiful hazel eyes. "Would you mind sitting in here for just a little while, maybe until I go to sleep?"

He hated the fear that darkened her eyes, the slight tremble of her lower lip. Those lips were made for laughing, for kissing, not for trembling with fear.

"I'll stay here as long as you want me to," he replied.

She took off her robe and laid it on the end of the bed, then slid in beneath the sheet. Caleb turned off the light and then sat on the edge of the bed.

The light from the hallway allowed him to see her face and even though she closed her eyes he saw the tension that rode her features and knew sleep wouldn't come easy for her. "Want to talk about it?" he asked softly.

She opened her eyes and looked at him. "I just wish somebody could tell me why this is happening, what I've done to deserve this."

"You don't deserve this, no matter what you might have done," he replied.

"Maybe this is the end of it," she said as her eyelids drooped with sleepiness. "Maybe after tonight whoever it is will give up and go away."

"Maybe," he agreed, although he was certain that wasn't the case.

He couldn't forget that the person who wanted to harm Portia had taken a chance tonight by attempting to get to her with somebody else in the house. That move smelled of desperation and mindless rage.

Caleb's stomach twisted into a cold, hard knot. As much as he'd like to assure her that he saw a swift and just ending to all this, he didn't. What he did see was darkness and danger and a cunning assailant with murder on the mind.

As Portia drifted off to sleep, fear twisted in Caleb's heart.

Portia awoke with a gasp, for a moment disoriented as she took in her surroundings. Then the events of the night before came crashing back into her mind. The intruder, the hands around her throat, the fight for her life—the horrible visions flashed like a horror movie and all she wanted to do was leave the theater.

You're safe, a voice whispered in the back of her head. She sat up and drew a deep steadying breath.

Her last memory before sleep had overtaken her was of Caleb's presence next to her on the bed.

Hopefully nobody saw him take her out of her house the night before. Hopefully nobody knew she was here. Surely she'd be safe now.

Although there was no clock in the room she could tell by the cast of the sun streaming through the window that it was late. The house was silent and she assumed that Caleb had probably left to go to work.

As she got out of bed her jaw ached and her throat hurt, but it was a manageable pain. She grabbed her robe and pulled it on, then left the bedroom with coffee on her mind.

She'd scarcely looked at her surroundings the night before and so as she entered the living room she gazed around with interest. There wasn't much to see.

In between a nondescript beige chair and matching sofa was a wooden table with a beige lamp. An entertainment center held a television and stereo system and on one shelf was the only thing that indicated who lived here. That shelf contained photos of the Grayson family.

She stepped closer, her heart constricting as she gazed at a picture of Caleb and Brittany. She couldn't imagine the pain the Grayson men were all going through as they wondered what had happened to their sister.

"Good morning."

She jumped as Caleb appeared in the kitchen doorway. "I didn't know you were here," she exclaimed. He motioned her into the kitchen and to a chair at the table. She glanced at the clock on the stove and saw that it was just after ten. "Shouldn't you be at work?"

"You are my work for now," he replied as he poured her a cup of coffee and set it in front of her. "In fact, you're going to be my work until we figure this all out."

She looked at him in dismay. "Oh, Caleb, I don't want to take you away from everything else you should be doing."

His eyes were almost black. "I don't want you alone now, Portia. I want you here with me until we figure out what's going on. Nobody but Layla knows you're here and that's the way I want to keep it."

"But that's crazy," she protested. "You need to be working on finding your sister. You can't just drop everything because of me."

"I can't do anything right now to help Brittany. We've reached a dead end at the moment." His voice rang with a hint of his agony. "Until that changes I can try to keep you safe from harm."

Portia wrapped her fingers around her coffee mug and gazed at him intently. "And you would go to all this trouble for anyone in town?"

"You're not anyone," he said. "You're somebody I

once loved, somebody I still care about although not in the same way I once did. Now what do you want for breakfast?"

"Nothing, I'm really not hungry," she replied. She wasn't sure why his words hurt her just a little bit. After all, she felt the same way about him. He was somebody she still cared about but not in the romantic, loving way she'd once felt.

She couldn't deny that there was a strong physical attraction to him, but that had nothing to do with love. The idea of being cooped up here with him for the next few days filled her with a sense of peace and a simmering sense of anticipation.

She had no doubt that Caleb would keep her safe from whoever wanted to do her harm, but she wasn't sure who would keep her safe from Caleb. And did she really want to be kept safe from him?

"I forgot to tell you, Joe Castle stopped by my house last night," she said in an attempt to banish thoughts of Caleb and sex from her mind.

His eyes narrowed and he sat in the chair next to hers. She caught his scent, a pleasant fragrance of minty soap and his familiar cologne. A flicker of desire lit in the pit of her stomach.

What was wrong with her? Her life had fallen apart, somebody wanted her dead and all she could think about was making love to Caleb. Maybe she was in some sort of shock, she thought.

"What did he want?" Caleb asked.

She took a sip of her coffee, hoping the warm liquid would banish her crazy thoughts. "He wanted to assure me that he had nothing to do with anything that's been happening to me. He was upset that I would even think him capable of doing anything to hurt me."

Caleb frowned. "Maybe I need to have another talk with him, find out where he was at two this morning."

She wanted to protest, to assure him that Joe couldn't have been the person who had crawled through her window, the person who had wrapped his hands around her throat and tried to squeeze the life from her. But she didn't. Other than Caleb and his brothers and Layla, she didn't know whom to trust in the town of Black Rock.

Portia finished her coffee and got up from the table. "I need to take a shower and get dressed for the day. What are the plans?"

"I'm going to get Benjamin to come over and sit for a while and I'm going to head over to Joe's and have a chat with him, then when I get back we'll go out and get some lunch."

"Surely I'll be okay here alone for a little while," she said halfheartedly. She hated taking another deputy away from his duties.

"You might be willing to gamble with your safety but I'm not," he said firmly. "Besides, it's our job to keep the people of Black Rock safe and Benjamin won't mind hanging out here with you. Now go shower, and I'm going to give Benjamin a call."

Even though she hated that she was being a burden on anyone, she was also relieved that Caleb wouldn't be leaving her all alone. Although she'd tried not to think about what had happened the night before, the truth was that the taste of terror still lingered in her mouth, still chilled her to her bones.

She didn't want to be alone for any length of time. She wanted small talk and somebody else's presence to keep away the fear that threatened to overwhelm her.

She felt better after a long, hot shower and dressed in a pair of white shorts and a bright yellow blouse. When she returned to the kitchen she was surprised to find Caleb already gone and Benjamin pouring himself a cup of coffee.

"Portia, you look surprisingly good for what you went through last night," he said in greeting.

She smiled and shook her head as he offered to pour her a cup of coffee. "No thanks, I'm jittery enough without too much caffeine."

There was definitely something reassuring about a man in a khaki uniform with a gun strapped to his hip. Portia had always liked Benjamin, who was soft-spoken and always pleasant.

"I appreciate you being here, Benjamin. But I hate that I'm taking you away from your job," she said as she sat at the table.

He smiled and sat in the chair opposite her. "This is my job," he replied, "although Caleb has taken this on like a personal crusade. I pity the perp if Caleb gets to him before any of the rest of us. Have you been able to think of anything else that you didn't tell us last night?"

She frowned and shook her head. "It all happened so fast and the room was so dark. I wish I would have thought to try to get that ski mask off."

"You were too busy trying to stay alive," he replied. "Sooner or later whoever it is will make a mistake and we'll get him."

"I hope it's sooner rather than later. I want my life back." And she wasn't at all sure she liked the idea of spending her days and nights here in Caleb's house, where his scent permeated everything and his presence reminded her of a passion she'd only experienced with him.

Benjamin leaned back in his chair and took a sip of his coffee, his warm brown eyes gazing at her over the rim of the cup. "You doing okay?"

She nodded. "I guess as well as can be expected. I'm just frustrated because I have no idea who's behind these attacks. Maybe it's one of those aliens Walt Tolliver is always talking about."

Benjamin laughed and then frowned thoughtfully. "Walt's always been an odd duck, but lately he seems to be more obsessed about an alien invasion than usual. I'm worried about him."

"I know his wife died three or four years ago. Does he have other family?" she asked.

"A granddaughter. Her name is Edie Burnett and she lives in Topeka. I called her yesterday and got her voice mail and left her a message to get back to me, but so far I haven't heard from her."

"It's still early. I'm sure you'll hear from her before the day is over."

"I hope so. I just want some family member to check in with him and make sure he's doing okay."

"You're a nice man, Benjamin. How come you aren't married?" she asked.

He wrapped his large hands around the coffee mug and smiled ruefully. "I'm a one-woman man and I guess I just haven't found my one woman yet. And I could ask you the same question. Why aren't you married with a bunch of your own kids running around?"

"Because I think loving Caleb ruined me for ever loving another man." She stared at him, appalled that she'd actually spoken those words aloud.

"Don't worry, I won't tell him what you said," he assured her with a soft smile. "And for what it's worth, I think maybe it's the same way for him."

"That's not true," she scoffed. "He apparently loved Laura Kincaid. They were engaged to be married."

Benjamin leaned back in his chair and once again frowned thoughtfully. "Whatever he had with Laura,

I don't think it was real love. He didn't have that sparkle in his eyes, that spring to his step that he always had when he was around you. When she left town he wasn't heartbroken. He was just angry. I think Caleb has been angry since the time you two broke up."

She leaned back in her chair and released a deep sigh. "Oh, Benjamin, Caleb's and my past is like a big white elephant in the room. We've never really talked about what happened and why. There's never been any real sense of closure between the two of us."

He smiled at her. "Then maybe it's time to get out the great big hunting gun and shoot down that elephant. Maybe what you two need is a second chance."

A whisper of warmth swept through her, the warmth of possibility. Could she and Caleb somehow move away from their past and find each other again? Was it possible they could have a second chance?

Almost immediately the warmth that had tried to take hold of her was overwhelmed by the chill of her reality as she remembered that somebody didn't want her to have a second chance. Somebody simply wanted her dead.

Chapter 9

It was just after one when Caleb pulled back in to his driveway. He parked the car but instead of getting out he leaned his head forward and released a weary sigh.

He was exhausted. Sleep had been nearly impossible after Portia had fallen asleep the night before. He'd sat on the edge of the bed and watched her as she'd slept and he'd admitted to himself the truth, that he did still care about her deeply.

He would have married Laura and he would have done his best to ensure that they had a happy life together, but his feelings for the pretty blonde had never been the same as what he'd felt for Portia.

He tried to tell himself that his intense attraction

to Portia was based on nothing more than memories of what had been, but he knew that wasn't completely true. In the last couple of days he'd come to admire her inner strength, had been reminded again and again by the people he'd interviewed of what a warm and loving woman she was, how much so many of the other people in town liked her. She was a good woman who deserved a good man, but he refused to consider that he might be that man.

He raised his head and got out of the car, the August sun scorching on his back. The idea of being cooped up with Portia in the house for the next couple of days made him feel just a little bit crazy.

How long could he smell her scent, see that occasional flicker of flame in her eyes, and not explode? How long could he see those lips of hers and not want to take them again in a kiss that left them both gasping and wanting?

More than anything he wanted to make love to her again and almost more than anything else in the world the very idea scared him. Although he was determined to keep her from walking into his heart, he was terrified that somehow she'd manage to slide in beneath his defenses.

He found her and his brother in the kitchen and seated at the table playing cards. "Thank God, you're back," Benjamin exclaimed as he scooted his chair back from the table. "She's a regular cardsharp. She's beat me nine games out of ten."

"Poker?" Caleb asked.

Portia grinned. "Go Fish."

Benjamin threw his cards on the table and stood. "What did you find out about Joe?"

"He left Portia's last night and hooked up with Ann Tyler. They had a few drinks at Harley's and then she went back to his place with him. I confirmed the story with Ann, who said Joe didn't leave his bed all night."

"So you're back to square one," Benjamin said.

"Unfortunately yes," Caleb agreed and fought to keep the frustration out of his voice.

"I'm heading back to the office. Is there anything else you need me to do?" Benjamin asked.

"It's too early for anything to have come in from the bedding we took last night." Caleb shook his head. "No, I guess there's nothing."

"Then I'll see you both later."

As Benjamin left, Caleb turned to Portia. "How about we head to the café for some lunch?"

"Should I be seen out in public?" she asked, a touch of fear darkening her beautiful eyes.

Caleb had been considering their next course of action since the moment he'd left the house earlier. He leaned with his hip against the counter and gazed at her intently. "Initially my first thought was to hide you here, to make sure that nobody knew you were here in an effort to keep you safe."

"And now?"

"And now I'm wondering if it's a better idea to let everyone in town know that you're staying here." He saw her eyes narrow and then widen in sudden comprehension.

"Use me as bait," she said. She reached up and tucked a strand of her hair behind one ear, and he noticed that her slender hand trembled slightly.

"It's your call, Portia. If I didn't think I could keep you safe, then I'd never suggest it in the first place," he said.

She frowned thoughtfully, her gaze never leaving his. "I trust you," she finally said. "Besides, it might be the only way to pull the person out of the shadows. I want this done and over and if this is the way to accomplish it, then I'm in."

"Then let's head to the café," he said. Two minutes in his kitchen with her alone and he was already eager to escape the small confines.

Minutes later they were in his car. "He presumably hung the flyers at night and slammed into your car on a dark, isolated road. Last night he hoped to find you asleep and vulnerable. I'm guessing that as long as you're out in the daylight and surrounded by other people you'll be safe," he said as he backed out of the driveway. "It's obvious he's not crazy enough to make an attack where somebody might be able to identify him."

"What makes you think he'll come after me at your house? I mean, it's one thing for him to think he could get to me with just Layla standing in the way, but it's another for him to think he can get past an armed deputy to get to me."

"We'll figure it out," he replied. "All I want to focus on now is a big juicy hamburger with extra pickles."

She smiled at him. "Remember that night you and I sat at your mother's kitchen table and you ate a whole jar of sweet pickles and she got so mad because she was going to use them to make potato salad?"

The memory pulled a burst of laughter to his lips. "She was so mad, she said I'd ruined the meal she was going to take the next day to poor Mrs. Whittaker, who was recovering from back surgery."

"You got a bellyache and poor Mrs. Whittaker got macaroni and cheese instead of your mom's signature potato salad." Her eyes sparkled in a way he hadn't seen for what seemed like a hundred years and that sparkle lit a flame of want deep inside him.

He focused on finding a parking place in front of the café. "Things seemed so easy then," he said as he pulled the car to a halt and cut the engine.

"We thought we had the world by the tail," she replied. "We were so young and so ridiculously arrogant."

"Yeah, we were." He opened the car door. "Let's go eat."

He didn't want to share memories with her. He didn't want to think about that time when he'd had her in his arms, in his heart, and it had felt right. He'd thought he'd known exactly what his future would be with her.

They entered the café and he spied an empty booth toward the back. He led her there and he took the side facing the door. If trouble walked into the café he wanted to see it instantly.

Immediately Linda the waitress arrived at their table with water glasses and menus. "I don't need one of those," Caleb said as Linda started to hand him one of the menus.

Linda smiled. "Let me guess, a big burger with no onions and extra pickles, curly fries and a soda."

"You've got it," he replied.

"And what about you, Portia? You good without a menu, too?" Linda asked.

"I'll have the same thing he's having and just put my pickles on his burger," she said.

"Got it," Linda said and left the booth.

Almost immediately an awkward silence descended between them. Caleb focused his attention around the café, trying to notice if anyone was paying them unusual attention. But he felt Portia's gaze lingering on him and finally returned his focus to her.

"Last night right before the person broke in through my window I was dreaming about prom night," she said.

Shock stuttered through him. Of all the things he'd

expected her to want to talk about, that night wasn't even on the list. "Oh, yeah?" he replied carefully.

She held his gaze with an intensity that stirred more than a little nervous tension inside him. "I was dreaming that we were on the bed in the motel room and you were unzipping my dress."

His throat went dry as he remembered the silk of her bare skin, the way her heart had beat a rapid tattoo against his own. "Why are you telling me this?" he asked, his voice holding a slightly rough edge even to his own ears.

"Because I think we need to talk about it, about us and what happened years ago," she replied. "I don't want it to be taboo between us anymore."

"There's nothing to talk about," he exclaimed. "We dated, we broke up, end of story. Most high school romances don't last. We weren't that different than a million other couples at that age."

"But I have things I want to talk about," she replied.

He glanced around the busy café and then looked back at her. "This isn't the time or the place for any kind of personal conversation. Let's just eat and then if you still want to we can talk about it later."

He hoped that she'd just forget whatever it was she thought she had to say. He didn't want to revisit any of it. There was no fixing it. What was done was done and he didn't even want to think about it, let alone talk about it.

Their lunch was delivered and the awkward silence that had appeared earlier returned between them. Caleb tried to keep his focus on the other people in the café rather than on the woman across from him.

Larry Norwood, the town vet, sat at the counter chatting with Margie Meadows, a tough-talking widow who worked at the convenience store at the edge of town. At a nearby table a bunch of high school–aged girls giggled and shot longing gazes to a handsome young man who sat alone at the counter.

He wanted to tell the young man to run hard and fast from teenage heartbreak, but knew that it was possible that teenage angst was a part of the painful rite of passage into adulthood.

They were nearly finished eating when Tom walked in. He spied Caleb and Portia and approached their booth. "Portia," he said in greeting. "How are you doing today?"

"Better than I was doing last night when you saw me," she replied.

"My little brother taking care of you okay?"

"Maybe too well. I feel more than a little guilty taking him away from other work."

Tom smiled, but the gesture didn't quite reach the darkness of his eyes. "Keeping you safe is his job."

"That's what I keep telling her," Caleb said.

"How're Peyton and Lilly doing?" Portia asked.

"They're great." Joy sparked in Tom's eyes and

despite Caleb's desire to remain alone, he felt a small touch of envy strike him.

"When are you going to make an honest woman out of Peyton?" Portia asked.

The light in Tom's eyes dimmed. "When Brittany is home and can attend the wedding," he replied.

"I pray that happens," she replied.

He nodded and focused back on Caleb. "You'll keep me posted on what's going on?"

"You know it," Caleb replied easily.

With a murmured goodbye Tom left them and sat at the counter next to Larry Norwood. "He's still optimistic that we're going to find Brittany alive and well," Caleb said. "But with each day that passes my hope of that happening is disappearing."

"I hope you're wrong and Tom is right," Portia said and shocked him by reaching across the table and taking Caleb's hand in hers.

Her fingers entwined with his and he couldn't help but think it was a perfect fit. He'd always loved to hold hands with her because her hand fit so neatly into his.

"You can't lose hope, Caleb," she said and her fingers tightened around his. "You have to believe that everything is going to be okay, that eventually we're all going to get a happy ending."

He pulled his hand from hers. "I don't believe in happy endings," he said curtly and got up from the booth. "You ready to go?"

She scooted out of the booth and together they went to the counter to pay. He'd just received his change when he heard her gasp his name.

He whirled around as she grabbed his arm in a death grip. "Dale Stemple," she managed to sputter. "He just went by driving a car. It was him, Caleb. I swear it was him."

Adrenaline pumped through him as he grabbed Portia by the arm and the two of them raced out of the café. This was the break he'd been waiting for, the break they had needed—proof positive that Dale Stemple was here in town.

Now all he had to do was find the man before he accomplished his goal of killing Portia.

Portia's heart pumped a million miles a minute as she jumped into Caleb's car. "Which way?" he asked and she pointed up the street to their right. "What kind of car?"

"It was a black sedan," she replied as she fumbled with her seat belt. The vision of Dale filled her head and created cold chills to creep up her spine. "It has to be him, Caleb. He's the only one who makes sense. None of this happened until he got out of prison."

Caleb started the car with a roar, and with its tires squealing out of the parking lot, they headed in the direction she'd indicated.

"You watch and see if you see the car parked

anywhere," Caleb instructed as he kept his gaze focused on the road ahead.

Portia scanned both sides of the road, seeking the car containing the man who at the moment she feared more than anyone else on the face of the earth. Shops whizzed by and she checked the parking spaces in front of them, but she didn't see the car anywhere.

Had he looked into the café window and seen her with Caleb? Had he followed them here from Caleb's after realizing she wasn't staying in her house anymore?

She clutched the seat on either side of her with her hands, an explosive tension ready to detonate at any moment.

Caleb drove to the edge of the town limits, where the highway cut in and it was impossible to discern which direction the car might have gone. He muttered a curse, slammed his palm down on the dashboard and then looked at her. "Are you sure it was him?"

"Positive." She couldn't fight the shiver that worked through her. "I'll never forget his face. I've thought about him since the moment you mentioned his name to me. It was him. I know it was him."

Caleb pulled a U-turn and went back the way they had come. "I don't know where he was going, but he has to be staying at his parents' house," he said. "I had some of the other deputies check the motel and I know he isn't staying there."

"He must hate me so much. I destroyed his life," Portia said.

Caleb shot her a quick glance as a muscle ticked in his taut jaw. "He destroyed his own life by beating his children and selling illegal guns. You saved those two kids from any more abuse. You should have gotten a damned medal for turning him in."

As he turned a corner the tension inside her rose again. "Where are we going?"

"To the Stemples.'" He held the steering wheel so tight his knuckles were white. "We're going to find out once and for all if Dale is there."

Although that was the very last place Portia wanted to go, she bit her tongue and kept silent. Caleb's hard expression forbade her from speaking any protest. She saw his determination in the slight thrust of his square chin, knew that look well enough to know that nothing was going to stop him from doing what he felt he needed to do.

"Don't be scared," he said as his hands loosened on the wheel.

"What makes you think I'm scared?"

He shot her a quicksilver grin. "Because you're about to claw your way through the seat."

She pulled her hands from the sides of the seat and into her lap. "Shouldn't you call for backup or something?"

"I've got it under control," he replied.

She hoped he did. The only thing that made her

relax slightly was the fact that Dale had been driving in the opposite direction.

When they pulled up in front of the Stemple house, there was no dark sedan parked in the driveway. "Come with me," Caleb said as he cut the engine. "I don't want you sitting in the car all alone."

The two of them got out of the car and she was grateful when he threw an arm around her shoulders as if to shield her from any danger that might suddenly appear.

When they reached the door Caleb gave it a three-knuckle rapid series of taps. He waited only a moment and then knocked again.

"All right, all right, hold your horses," a deep voice came from inside. The door opened and Dale's father, Art Stemple, frowned as he saw the two of them on his porch. "Caleb, Ms. Perez, what can I do for you folks?"

Portia had seen Dale's parents around town since Dale's arrest, but Art Stemple looked as if he'd aged ten years since the last time she'd seen him. Deep lines cut through his face and he looked old and frail.

"Art, we need to talk to Dale," Caleb said. "We know he's in town and I know he's been staying here."

Caleb's words were a lie. They didn't know any such thing. Although Portia was certain that Dale was in town, for all they knew he could be staying at a friend's place, living in his car or using an alias and staying in a nearby town.

Art's cheeks reddened. "I already told you he wasn't here and that we haven't heard from him since he got out of prison. I don't know why you keep bothering me about this."

"So you wouldn't mind if we came inside and took a look around," Caleb said.

Art's frown deepened as he drew himself up straighter. "I've never had problems with you or any of your brothers, Caleb. I've been a law-abiding citizen all my life, but if you want to come inside and look around then you're going to have to bring me a search warrant and that's all I've got to say on the matter."

Before Caleb could speak again, Art closed the door and Portia heard the distinct click of a lock turning. Caleb once again threw his arm around her shoulders as they walked back to his car.

"There's no doubt in my mind that he's staying here," he said as they pulled out of the Stemple driveway and headed back to Caleb's house.

"How can you be sure?"

He frowned. "I can't be, but I swear when Art opened his door I smelled the faint odor of cigarette smoke. I know Art and his wife don't smoke, but if I remember right, Dale did."

"Like a chimney," she agreed.

"Unfortunately, there's no way I can get a search

warrant without any evidence that he's committed a crime. As far as the law is concerned he served his time and is a free man."

"So what do we do now?" she asked.

"We go back to my place and I make some phone calls. I want to see if I can get Tom to agree to putting some men on surveillance at the Stemple place. Dale might not have been there now, but eventually he'll come back and we can at least bring him in for questioning. We can't lose sight of the fact that it's still possible that somebody else is behind all this."

"I don't think so," she replied. "He's the only one who makes sense. He has a reason to hate me and I wasn't having any problems before he got released from prison."

"Trust me, Dale is at the top of my suspect list."

She could tell that he was far away from her, deep in thoughts of how best to find resolution for her problems.

She'd been disappointed that he'd halted the conversation she'd wanted to have with him about their past. She suspected that with all that had happened since then he probably thought she'd forgotten about it, but she hadn't. Sooner or later she was going to have that conversation with him and admit to him that she might have made a mistake.

I think Caleb has been angry since the two of you broke up. Benjamin's words came back to her. If what he'd said was true, then Caleb's anger implied a lack of closure and perhaps a depth of emotion where she was concerned that she hadn't known he was capable of feeling.

She glanced at him now, noting the strong line of his jaw, the sensual lips that had always driven her half-insane. She'd compared every man she'd ever dated to Caleb and each and every one of them had come up short.

Within minutes they were back in the house. Caleb immediately excused himself and disappeared with his cell phone into his bedroom.

Portia went into the guest bedroom and sat on the edge of the bed. Even though she'd slept late, the events of the previous night, coupled with the trauma of seeing Dale again, shot a weighty weariness through her.

Maybe she'd feel better if she took a little nap. She stretched out on the bed and closed her eyes, but a million visions danced in her brain.

Memories of prom night and making love to Caleb whispered through her, bringing with them a heat of desire. She wanted him. She thought she might always want him, but he'd made it fairly clear that if they did make love again it would just be sex, not anything meaningful for him.

Could she live with that? One more time in Caleb's arms, one more time feeling his body moving with hers, and not want more from him? She didn't know.

She closed her eyes and a vision of Dale leaped into her brain. Tension coiled tight inside her as she thought of the man she believed wanted her dead.

Dale wasn't a big man. Rather he had the wiry build of a street scrapper. Some women would find him attractive, with his black hair and piercing blue eyes. The few times she'd seen him, what she'd noticed was the sense of imminent explosion that clung to him, an aura that whispered of hidden danger.

She thought of the person who had attacked her in her bedroom. Had it been Dale? It was definitely possible. The person hadn't been huge, although in the dark of night and with the weight of her fear, the person had been as big as a monster.

Where would this all end? Would Caleb and the rest of the team of deputies be able to keep her safe, to get Dale arrested and back in prison where he belonged?

And how long would she have to live her life in limbo? How long before she could get back to her own home, back to her work and the children that she loved?

As she thought of the kids a raw emotion crawled up the back of her throat and no matter how hard she swallowed against it she couldn't dislodge it.

Tears stung her eyes as she thought of the babies who were such an integral part of her life. When was she going to see them all again? When would she be able to hug and kiss them, tell stories and watch their little faces light up with joy?

A sob welled up inside her, impossible to contain. She rolled over on her tummy and buried her head into her pillow as the tears began to flow in earnest.

Deep, wrenching sobs overwhelmed her. She cried because she missed her kids, because somebody hated her enough to kill her and finally her tears were for the love that had been lost so many years ago.

A soft knock on the door couldn't stop her weeping. "Portia?" The door opened and she was aware of Caleb entering the room.

"Go away," she said, the words choking out of her on a new sob.

"What's wrong?" The bed depressed with his weight. "Why are you crying?"

"Because I feel like it," she said, knowing she sounded childish but unable to help it.

He laid a hand on her shoulder. "Don't. We'll get this all sorted out. Please stop, you know I could never stand it when you cried." His hand moved in a circular motion on her shoulder blade. "What brought all this on?"

"I miss my kids. I miss my life," she said as the tears began to ebb.

"You'll get it back," he assured her as his hand moved lower, stroking from her shoulder blade to the center of her back. "You just have to be strong a little while longer."

"I don't feel very strong right now." As she turned over he pulled his hand away. She sat up and shoved her hair away from her face. "I'm feeling very weak right now."

For a moment his gaze locked with hers and a new tension twisted inside her. He opened his arms and pulled her against his chest. "Then I'll be strong for you," he murmured against her hair.

She melted against his strong chest, for the first time in days feeling one hundred percent safe. His hands smoothed up and down her back and she burrowed closer against him, wishing she could remain in his arms until Dale Stemple was behind bars.

She had no idea how long they remained like that, and nothing else would have happened if he hadn't pressed his lips against her temple, if he hadn't stroked his hand down to her hip.

A fire lit inside her, one that she knew only he could put out. She didn't care about consequences or promises. She just wanted him right now in this very moment.

She leaned back from him just enough to capture his mouth with hers. He met the kiss with eager greed, their tongues meeting and swirling together as fire torched through her.

The kiss lingered until they were both breathless and when he finally pulled away from her, his eyes glowed with a heat that threatened to melt her into a puddle.

He didn't say a word. He stood from the bed and held his hand out to her. She knew he intended to take her into his bedroom and make love to her. She saw his intention in the depths of his eyes, in the tension that held him rigidly in place.

She had only a moment in which she knew she could halt things before they flared out of control, a single second to decide if she wanted to listen to her head or her heart.

There was really no decision to be made, she thought. With a sweet anticipation winging through her, she stood and took his hand.

Chapter 10

Caleb's heart thundered as he led her down the hallway to his bedroom. He knew what they were about to do was stupid, but he felt drunk and reckless with his need for her.

Somebody's hand trembled but he wasn't sure if it was hers or his own. He felt a tremor through his entire body, a tremor of anticipation.

They reached his bedroom, where the sun shimmered in through the window filtered by the thick leaves of a maple tree just outside. He dropped her hand when they were next to his bed.

For a long moment he just drank in her beauty. Dappled by shadow and sunlight, her eyes shone with desire and her breasts rose and fell with her quickened breaths.

He was afraid to speak, almost afraid to move, worried that the moment would be shattered and she'd change her mind and walk away.

He held his breath as she stepped closer to him and her fingers went to the buttons on his shirt. She caught her lower lip between her teeth as she began to unfasten the buttons, her gaze focused on the task rather than looking up at him.

Remaining perfectly still, he felt his arousal start in the crash of his heartbeat, the fever that seemed to sweep over him and the uncomfortable tightening of his khaki slacks.

As she reached the last of the buttons, she finally looked up at him as she pulled the shirt from his shoulders and allowed it to fall to the floor.

He couldn't remain still another minute. He pulled her roughly against him and once again took her mouth with his. She tasted like half-remembered sin, like youth and desire. It was a taste he'd never forgotten, would never forget.

As the kiss continued he began to unfasten the buttons that ran down the front of her blouse. He began slowly but by the time he reached the last button his fingers were clumsy with haste.

The blouse fell away, leaving her in her bra. With her gaze still locked with his, she unzipped her white shorts and slid them down the length of her legs.

Both her panties and her bra were plain, no lace or frills, just sturdy white cotton that Caleb found sexier than anything he'd ever seen in his life.

"You're so beautiful. You take my breath away," he whispered.

A blush swept into her cheeks and she shook her head as if to negate his words. That had always been part of Portia's charm, that she didn't recognize just how beautiful she was.

As she got into the bed he took off his shoes, socks and slacks and then joined her. He took her into his arms, relishing his bare skin against her, but impatient with the underwear that kept them from being completely naked with each other.

No old memories of prom night intruded into his mind. He was firmly in the here and now and making love to Portia the woman, not Portia the inexperienced teenager.

As he kissed her again he wound his arms around her and unfastened her bra, eager to feel the weight of her breasts in his palms, taste her nipples as they pebbled with pleasure in his mouth.

He pulled the bra from her and slid his lips down the length of her neck. Her hands wound in his hair, fastening there and pulling slightly in anticipation of his mouth sliding down her body.

She whispered his name as his hands cupped her breasts and his tongue flicked at one of the erect nipples. She moved beneath him, twining her slender legs with his as he continued to tease and kiss first one nipple and then the other.

Her hands untangled from his hair and smoothed down the length of his back, sparking electric sizzles with each touch.

He was ready to take her, swollen and half-mindless with the need to plunge into her, but in the part of his mind that still worked rationally he knew he'd be cheating her by moving too fast.

"Caleb," she whispered and he raised his head to look at her. "I want us naked," she said, as if she'd read his mind, as if she knew his need.

"Me, too," he said. He rolled away from her and tore off his briefs at the same time she removed her panties. When they came back together his body ached with the feel of her nakedness against his.

He slid his hand up her inner thigh, heard the slight gasp of pleasure that she released as his fingers found her heat.

She arched her hips up to meet him and, at the same time, wound her fingers around the hard length of him. Intense pleasure crashed through him as she moved her hand up and down. She seemed to know just how much pressure to use, what kind of touch evoked the sharpest response.

He wanted, needed to take her over the edge before he found his own release. He gently pushed her hand away from him so he focused completely on bringing her as much pleasure as possible.

As he continued to stroke her intimately, he felt the rising tension in her. Her breathing grew more rapid and she began to moan, the deep, throaty sound increasing his desire. Her legs tensed and she cried out his name as he brought her to climax.

Almost immediately he rolled away from her and fumbled in his nightstand drawer for a condom. He ripped the foil package with more force than necessary and rolled the protection into place.

She was ready for him as he eased between her thighs and entered her. She welcomed him by clutching his buttocks and pulling him deep within.

He closed his eyes and refused to move, afraid that if he did it would be over before it began. They fit together as perfectly as they had years ago and the scent of her, the familiar contours of her body against his, caused a wealth of emotions to crash through him, emotions that had nothing to do with the physical act itself.

He opened his eyes and looked down at her, surprised that her features swam as tears filled his eyes. She, too, had tears glittering in her eyes. He quickly closed his again and began to move his hips against her.

She moaned again and it was a sound that stole all thought from his mind. He stroked into her faster and faster and felt her tightening around him as she once again reached her peak.

As she cried out and shuddered, he climaxed, the force of it stealing every breath from his body. For a long moment they remained unmoving, gasping for breath, then he crashed to his back next to her, the only sound in the room their efforts to find a normal beat of their hearts.

"Wow," she finally said.

"My sentiments exactly," he replied. He closed his eyes for a moment, willing the emotions that had momentarily gripped him away.

He got out of the bed and padded into the bathroom and almost immediately was struck with a thousand kinds of regret.

He washed up and then stood in front of the mirror over the sink and stared at his reflection. "What the hell are you doing?" he asked the man in the mirror.

This was going to end badly. The emotions he felt for Portia scared the hell out of him. Portia was everything he desired and everything he refused to have in his life. Making love to her now had been one of the biggest mistakes of his life.

As always a knot of anger twisted in his gut. Twice he'd put his heart on the line for a woman and both times it had been trampled into the ground. He'd be a fool to put his heart out there again.

Caleb was a man meant to be alone and even though making love to Portia had been beyond wonderful, it didn't change his mind.

He returned to the bedroom and was slightly disappointed that she hadn't gotten dressed but rather remained naked in his bed. He grabbed his slacks from the floor as she sat up and clutched the sheet to her breasts.

"Caleb, we need to talk."

"Why? Portia, what we just did was pretty stupid." He pulled on his pants and refused to look at her, afraid that he would do something even more stupid.

"Funny, I don't feel stupid," she replied.

A wave of shame swept over him as he heard the faint tinge of hurt in her voice. He sat on the edge of the bed and looked at her. She looked incredibly hot even with the faint bruising around her throat and the red area on her jaw. "Sorry, I'm being a jerk."

She smiled. "Yes, you are, but you get points for recognizing it."

"I just don't want you to make this into something bigger than it is," he said and reached down to grab his shirt.

"Don't worry, I'm not planning my wedding announcements. I don't even know if I'll be alive tomorrow. I don't want to talk about the future, Caleb. I want to talk about the past."

"Why? We can't go back and change anything." He tensed, wishing she would just leave it alone.

"You're right, I can't change anything, but I can tell you that I was wrong not to believe you. I was wrong not to trust you. I allowed gossip and innuendo to screw up my head."

He hadn't realized how much he'd wanted, needed to hear that from her until now. It was as if he'd carried a weight with him for the past ten years and her words finally banished it.

"That night that you were out of town for your grandfather's funeral I went to the café to hang out with a bunch of kids. Jayme Cordell was there alone and I sat in a booth with her. It wasn't a big deal. In fact, I spent the whole night telling her all about you, about how much I missed you and how I knew you were the right girl for me."

He looked toward the window where the sun had disappeared. The forecast that morning had been for hot and humid and with a chance of late-afternoon thunderstorms, but the weather was the last thing on his mind as he gazed back at the woman he'd once loved with all his heart, with all his soul.

"It was nothing but innocent conversation and to tell the truth I think I bored her to death with all my talk about you. When I decided to head home she left the café, too. I walked her to her car and I guess enough people saw us leaving together that they got the wrong impression."

"And I heard the gossip and thought the worst." She frowned, the gesture doing nothing to detract from her loveliness. "It didn't help that I had my mother pounding it into my brain that all men were alike, that all of them were cheaters. I heard the rumors and instantly believed them."

She left the bed, magnificent in her nakedness, and crouched down in front of him. "I'm sorry, Caleb. I'm sorry that I hurt you, that I screwed things up between us. That's what I wanted to tell you."

He wanted to kiss her again. He wanted to take her back into his bed and make love to her all over again, with the weight of anger gone from his chest. But his head refused to allow him what his heart desired.

"Thank you for telling me that," he said. "And now I need to go make some phone calls and see what we can do to catch the man who wants you dead."

He didn't know what she expected from him, but he could tell by her expression that this wasn't it. She gracefully rose to her feet and moved away from him.

He left the room without a backward glance.

A rumble of thunder accompanied Portia as she left the guest room after she'd showered and dressed. Caleb was on the phone in the kitchen and she curled up on the sofa with only her thoughts as company and her cell phone in her hand.

She needed to call her mother. It was possible that the story of the break-in at Portia's house had made its way around the town. Doris would be worried if she couldn't get hold of her daughter.

She punched in the number that would connect

her to her mother and steeled herself for the conversation to come. "Hi, Mom," she said when Doris answered.

"I was wondering when I was going to hear from you," Doris said. "I heard there was trouble at your place last night. Where are you now?"

"I'm staying with Caleb. He'll keep me safe from whoever is after me."

There was a long pause. "And who is keeping you safe from that womanizing man?"

With her heart still filled with the lovemaking she and Caleb had just shared, with her head still reeling from the brief discussion they'd had, Doris's words aggravated Portia to the breaking point.

"Stop it, Mom," she exclaimed with a harsh tone. "If you can't say anything nice, then just don't talk. I'm sorry Dad left you years ago and I'm sorry you never got over it, but that doesn't mean that all men are bad. Your bitterness has driven everyone out of your life except me, and if you continue, you'll end up driving me away, too."

"I didn't raise you to talk to me that way," Doris said, but her voice was filled with more hurt than anger.

Portia drew a deep, steadying breath. "I love you, Mom, but I won't let you beat up on Caleb or any other man I might date. I won't let you ruin what happiness I might find with your bitterness."

"I love you, too, Portia. I just don't want you to get hurt. I don't want you to go through what I did."

"I won't, Mom. Oh, I might get hurt, but I'll never allow any heartbreak to keep me from seeking happiness again." She softened her voice. "You have to let it go. You have to let your bitterness go, Mom."

There was another long silence. "I'll think about what you said," Doris said grudgingly. "Although after all these years I'm not sure I know how to begin to do that."

"I just wanted to let you know that I'm all right, that I love you and I'll talk to you later." Portia hung up as Caleb came into the room.

"Everything all right?" he asked.

"Yes, I was just checking in with my mother. I knew she'd be worried."

Caleb sat on the opposite end of the sofa from her. "I checked in with Sam McCain. He's been sitting on the Stemple place since we left earlier but there's been no sign of Dale. When Sam's shift is over Dan Walker is going to take over and continue surveillance."

"Maybe he's staying someplace else around town," she said. "Maybe he has a friend or a relative we don't know about."

"It's possible, but I still think he's been staying at his parents' place. Art acted shady, like a man who was hiding something, and I know I smelled cigarette smoke."

"But we still can't be a hundred percent sure it's Dale who is after me," she said.

"True, but it doesn't matter who it is, I just want them under arrest." A rumble of thunder sounded overhead and the room got increasingly darker. Caleb got up from the sofa and went to the window. "Going to storm," he said.

"We could use some rain." She watched him as he remained staring outside. His shoulders were rigidly straight with tension and when he'd come out of the kitchen his eyes had held a guarded expression that brooked no intrusion.

Her heart expanded with an emotion she'd tried to deny, but in that moment she was faced with the truth. She was still as deeply, as profoundly in love with him as she had been years ago.

The knowledge didn't surprise her; it only sent a small edge of pain through her.

She'd hoped that by making love with him again, by telling him that she'd made a mistake before, that somehow he'd profess his love for her, but that hadn't happened. The only thing it had managed to do was broaden the distance between them.

There were moments she felt his love, saw it shining from his unguarded eyes, felt it in his simplest touch, but there was also an inexplicable darkness, an anger in him that she didn't understand.

"Tell me about Laura," she said.

He turned from the window and looked at her, the

dark shutters in his eyes firmly in place. "Why do you want to know about her?"

"Because she's a part of your past. Because I'm curious."

"We dated, we broke up, end of story." He shrugged as if to dismiss the issue, but there was something raw and unbridled in his voice that let her know there was far more to the story.

"She hurt you," Portia said softly. His jaw tensed as his mouth compressed into a thin slash. "You must have loved her very much," Portia added.

A burst of laughter left him, the sound bitter and harsh. "I'm not sure love had anything to do with it." He sighed and moved away from the window at the same time thunder rumbled once again.

He sat in the chair opposite the sofa and gazed at her for a long moment as if deciding whether to say more or not.

"It was nothing but lust that Laura and I initially shared," he finally said. "She told me she wasn't looking for anything permanent and neither was I, so we started dating with no expectations of it going any further than that."

He paused and broke his eye contact with her, instead focusing on the wall over the sofa as the room darkened with the storm overhead. "We'd been dating about four months when she came to me and told me she was pregnant. We'd gotten careless one night and apparently it hadn't been without consequence."

Portia's heart twisted in her chest. Laura had been pregnant? Did Caleb have a son someplace? Maybe a daughter whom Laura had taken away from him? Certainly that would explain the anger Caleb seemed to carry.

"Even though I didn't love Laura, I cared about her and I thought love would come so I asked her to marry me. The idea of being a father blew me away. I wanted that more than anything I've ever wanted in my life." His hands clenched into fists at his sides. "I had it all figured out. I knew I'd be an awesome dad and I could make myself be a good husband."

"So you and Laura got engaged," Portia said.

He nodded. "And as we planned the wedding I committed myself and my heart to Laura and the baby. It was going to be a quick, simple wedding. I wanted it to happen before the baby arrived. Family has always been important to me and I was determined that we'd be a happy family. The wedding was all set for a Sunday afternoon a month away when she came to me and told me she couldn't go through with it."

A flash of lightning lit the room, followed closely by a thunderclap that shook the windows in their frames. Portia jumped but stayed focused on Caleb, whose features were tortured by incredible pain.

"She left and you don't know where your child is?" Portia asked, guessing that's what had happened.

Again that bitter laughter burst from him, shooting

an arrow of sympathy for him through her heart. "No. I wish that's what had happened. She not only didn't want to marry me. She didn't want to have my baby. She aborted it without telling me."

"Oh." The single word leaped to Portia's lips as tears blurred her vision. She couldn't stay on the sofa with him across the room, his heartache so big it filled the entire house.

As she got up and walked toward him, her tears spilled down her cheeks. His grief burned hot and painful in her throat as he stood, his body vibrating with emotion.

She wrapped her arms around his neck, vaguely surprised when he didn't push her away but rather gathered her close to him.

As she began to cry harder he held her by her shoulders and looked at her. "Why are you crying?" he asked.

"For you, Caleb. I'm crying for what you lost and because I wish it would have been me who was carrying your baby. I'm crying because I would have cherished your child."

He pulled her against him once again and outside the storm unleashed itself, pelting rain against the windows as they grieved for what might have been.

Chapter 11

He had to get her out of his house, Caleb thought three days later as he stood at the kitchen window to drink his morning coffee. Portia was still asleep and he relished this moment that held no tension.

Every since he'd told Portia about Laura's betrayal he'd felt vulnerable and had compensated by keeping his distance, which had created a nearly impossible, uncomfortable tension between himself and Portia.

For the past three days they had been in a wait-and-see pattern, waiting for Dale or whoever was after Portia to make his next move, wondering if and when another attack might come.

It was time to take the game to the next level. He knew the person who wanted to harm her was just waiting for the right opportunity to strike, and tonight Caleb intended to present that opportunity.

It was a dangerous gamble, but he couldn't allow things to go on as they had any longer. She'd touched him too deeply with her tears for him. She'd floored him with her statement that she'd wished she'd been pregnant with his child. She was getting beneath his defenses and he couldn't allow that to happen.

It was time for action, but the risk he was going to take made him feel slightly sick to his stomach. If anything went wrong, if anything happened to Portia, he didn't know how he would ever be able to live with himself.

"Good morning."

He whirled around from the window at the sound of her voice. "Good morning," he replied. "Coffee's made."

She was already dressed for the day in a turquoise sundress that made her eyes more blue than green. She poured herself a cup of coffee and sat at the table. "I think it's time I find another place to stay," she said.

He looked at her in surprise. "And where would that be? Who could keep you as safe as me?"

"I don't know, but we can't go on like this. I can't handle the tension anymore. Besides, I can't stay here forever and it doesn't look like anything is going to happen while I'm here."

"I know, and that's why I think it's time to up the

stakes." He joined her at the table and his heart beat just a little bit faster as he thought of the plan he'd spent half the night going over in his mind.

"Up the stakes how?" She curled her fingers around her coffee cup, as if his words had created a chill she needed to banish.

"I think probably our potential killer has been watching the house. By now everyone in town knows you're staying here, so he knows that, as well. My car has been parked in front the whole time so he knows I've been with you every minute of the day and night. I think whoever is after you is nearby. It's just my gut instinct, but my gut is rarely wrong," Caleb said.

"So, what's your plan?" she asked.

She was so beautiful with the morning light splashing on her features, and a new fear clutched his guts as he leaned back in the chair and eyed her intently.

"After dark tonight I'm going to drive away. Benjamin will sneak into the backyard and hide. He can move like a shadow in the dark and hopefully the perp won't see him taking his place. I'll park and come back to hide in the front yard. We'll keep the house under surveillance and see if Dale or whoever shows up, and if he does we'll have him arrested before he can do anything to hurt you."

"What if he isn't watching the house tonight?" she asked.

"Then we'll do the same thing tomorrow night

and the night after that. Eventually he'll be here to see my car gone and he'll assume that you're here by yourself."

"And if this doesn't work? What if he's too smart to take the bait?" she asked.

"Then we come up with another plan." He leaned forward. "But I think he hates you more than he has sense."

"Gosh, that makes me feel warm and fuzzy," she said dryly.

"Portia, we won't go through with this if you don't want to. I want you to understand that with any plan there's risk, but I believe the risk in this case is minimal." God, at least he hoped the risk was minimal. He'd worked and reworked it around in his head, afraid to go through with it and yet afraid not to try.

She frowned thoughtfully and turned her head to gaze out the window. "I'm so tired of being afraid. I'm tired of my life being on hold." She raised her chin and looked at him once again. "Let's do it. I want this ended and if that can happen tonight, then let's get it over and done."

He nodded and hoped that he wasn't making a mistake. They ate a silent breakfast, each lost in their own thoughts, and then Caleb took the phone back to his bedroom and called Benjamin to set up the plans for the night.

The afternoon stretched into evening with first

Portia pacing the living room and then Caleb restlessly walking from room to room.

At six-thirty they sat down to a dinner of baked chicken and rice that Portia had prepared. Although Caleb's stomach was twisted into too many knots for him to feel hungry, he forced himself to eat.

Portia picked at the food on her plate, as if she had no appetite, as well. He wished he could tell her that everything was going to be all right, that by this time tomorrow night she'd be back home with her world once again as it should be, but he couldn't.

He had no idea what the night might bring. It was possible that whoever was after her wouldn't show up, wouldn't take the bait. Caleb would give it three nights and if nothing happened then maybe it was time they considered other arrangements for Portia.

If she continued to stay in his house he was afraid they'd make love again, he was terrified that he'd forget his own commitment to remain alone. Ultimately he was afraid that he'd be hurt again and he couldn't allow that to happen.

She released a sigh and shoved her plate away. "I can't eat. I have too many things on my mind."

He didn't ask her what things, afraid of what she might say. Since the night they'd made love he'd felt emotions coming off her that he didn't want to feel, knew that it was possible she had fallen for him again.

"Caleb, whatever happens tonight I want you to know that I'm thankful for everything you've done for me," she said.

"You can thank me after we have our bad guy behind bars," he replied.

"I'm almost grateful we had this time together. We needed a healing between us." Her eyes shone bright as she gazed at him. "I hope there has been a healing, that you forgive me for being young and foolish and easily influenced years ago."

A lump crawled into the back of his throat. "It was a long time ago, Portia." He pushed his plate to the side and thought about how devastated, how angry he'd been when she'd cast him out of her life.

He tried to summon that anger now, to use it as a shield against her, but no matter how hard he tried he couldn't get it back. All he felt was a profound sadness and the acceptance that it had never been in the cards that they would be together.

"I don't hold a grudge," he finally said. "I always knew how your mother was and that she had to have influenced your decision to break up with me."

"I can't put all the blame on my mother," she replied. "I should have trusted my heart where you were concerned instead of letting other people get inside my head."

"And maybe I should have fought harder to make you believe me," he replied. "I'm glad we talked about it, but it's just a part of my past now." These last words were said as a reminder to her and to himself that she had no place in his future.

She got up from the table and carried her plate to the sink and then she turned back to face him. "I'm going to go get my things packed up. If this goes the way we want it to, then I'll be ready to go back home immediately." She hesitated a moment, as if waiting for him to say something, but he merely nodded and she left the kitchen.

He stared out the window where the first edges of dusk were beginning to appear. The shadows at the base of the trees deepened with each passing moment and his heartbeat stirred a little faster as he realized it would soon be time to put his plan into action.

He grabbed his cell phone from his pocket and called Benjamin to double-check things. When he ended the call he once again looked out the window. There were plenty of places for Benjamin to hide in the backyard and still keep an eye on the house. The same was true of the front yard.

There was a full moon that night and the sky had been cloudless all day. The moonlight would aid them but make it more difficult for them to stay hidden to whoever might approach the house. But he was confident they would manage to cling to the shadows and stay out of sight.

It was a remarkably easy plan and no matter how Caleb twisted and turned he couldn't find any weaknesses that might lead to disaster. If somebody wanted to harm Portia tonight there was no question in his mind that either he or Benjamin could take him down before he even got close to her.

By eight-thirty, dusk had begun to transform to darkness. Caleb stood at the window and Brittany filled his mind.

An aching emptiness seeped into him at thoughts of his missing sister. Caleb and his brothers and the rest of the town of Black Rock had done everything they could to find her. The case had gone cold and the Grayson men were left wondering what they might have missed, what they could have done differently.

Knots of tension formed in the pit of his stomach. At the moment he felt as if they had already lost Brittany. He couldn't lose Portia, as well. He was aware that this plan had risks, but he believed they were minimal. Dammit, it had to work. It had to flush out the bad guy and give Portia back her life. And then he could get back to his own life, whatever it might be.

Darkness had fallen completely when he sensed Portia behind him. "It's almost time, isn't it?" she asked.

He turned to look at her. "Changed your mind?"

"No, I'm just ready to get this night over with. I want this person in jail and if taking a chance like this accomplishes it, then let's get on with it."

He fought the impulse to pull her against him,

to whisk her back into the bedroom and make love to her one last time. Instead he looked at his watch. "I'm going to move the car down the street about a block. Benjamin should be in position in the backyard by now. I'll park the car and then double back here. Benjamin will watch the back of the house and I'll watch the front and hopefully with my car gone, our perp will believe you're here all alone."

"Okay," she said, her voice reedy with nerves. Her eyes were huge and her lower lip trembled with anxiety.

"Don't be afraid," he said.

She offered him a forced, brave smile. "What makes you think I'm afraid?"

"I can hear your knees knocking together," he said.

She laughed and in that moment she looked more beautiful than he'd ever seen her and a sweet, haunting desire filled him.

Without thought, he grabbed her to him and captured her trembling lips with his own. He knew it was a stupid move, but he wanted one last embrace, one final kiss before he finally told her goodbye.

She wound her arms around his neck and clung to him as if he were her lifeline and for just a moment she felt like his.

He wanted to lose himself in her arms, kiss her forever, but, aware that it was time to go, he reluctantly stepped away from her.

"Lock the door behind me and I'll see you around dawn," he said as he opened the door. "Or earlier if our plan works."

He left the house and heard her lock the door behind him. He'd just pulled his keys from his pocket and unlocked the car door when his cell phone vibrated in his pocket.

He grabbed it and saw from the lighted caller ID that it was Benjamin. "Yeah?" he answered in a hushed tone as he stepped off the front porch.

"Tom called me to a car accident out on the highway. I'm just leaving now, but I wanted you to know I'll be about ten or fifteen minutes late," Benjamin said.

Caleb frowned. He'd assumed his brother was already in place. "I was just going to move my car in front of the Johnsons' place," he whispered in case an intruder was within earshot. "We get called there so often I figured it wouldn't look too suspicious parked there, but now I'll go back inside and wait for you to get into place. Call me back when you're in the backyard."

"Got it," Benjamin replied and then clicked off.

The Johnson family had two teenage boys that were often in trouble and at least once a month they responded to neighbor complaints about loud music or parties. Nobody would think it odd that two patrol cars were parked in front of that house.

Caleb would miss her. The thought stunned him.

In the time Portia had spent in his home she'd filled it with color and meaning. She'd made it feel like more than a place to sleep. She'd made it feel like a home.

He'd liked seeing her first thing in the morning and that she had been the last person he'd see before going to sleep at night. He liked the small talk he'd shared with her, the way her eyes lit up when she was tickled about something.

Yes, he'd liked having her with him—too much. And now he needed her away from him, back to her own life so that he could get back to his.

He'd give this plan three nights and then he'd have to figure out something else. Maybe he could move Portia into the cabin with Jacob. That way she'd be out of his house and still protected.

He couldn't help the small smile that crossed his lips as he thought of how irritated Jacob would be to have his isolation broken by Portia's presence.

His smile lingered only a minute and then fell as he pocketed his cell phone. He was just about to head back into the house when he heard a scrape behind him…the sound of a footstep on the concrete drive.

He started to whirl around but something hard smashed into the side of his head. Pain exploded in a cascade of pinpoint stars as he staggered back from the car.

As he fell, he had a moment of panic, of knowledge that Portia was in danger. He caught a glimpse of who had struck him, shocked that it hadn't been Dale Stemple or any of the people on their short list of suspects. Then darkness roared out and grabbed him.

The minute Caleb left, Portia headed for the kitchen to make herself a cup of hot tea. She was chilled to the bone and achingly aware of the fact for the next five minutes or so she was here alone and potentially vulnerable.

Before reaching the kitchen she walked over to the bookcase and looked at the photos on the shelves and her gaze lingered on Caleb's picture.

Love filled her, along with sadness. How long would it take her to get over this round with Caleb? It had taken her a long time to get over him when they'd broken up long ago. The truth was she'd never really gotten over him.

She sighed and went into the kitchen to fix herself the tea, hoping that would keep her awake until dawn and Caleb's eventual return into the house.

Caleb. As she filled the teakettle with water she continued thinking about him. She'd spent the last three days fighting the need to tell him how she felt about him. She wanted a second chance with him, an opportunity to get it right, but she was afraid that he didn't want the same thing.

There was no question that he wanted her on a physical level and she didn't doubt that he cared about her. There were moments when she felt his gaze on her that she thought she saw love in his eyes, but wondered if it was just her wishful thinking.

As she waited for the water to boil she glanced at the clock. It had only been minutes since he'd walked out the door. Was he already in place, hiding in the shrubs in the front of her yard or maybe across the street in her neighbor's yard?

Was Benjamin watching the back of her house, waiting for a potential killer to appear? This night would be endless. And what if it didn't yield the desired results?

She couldn't stay here much longer. Each and every minute she stayed in this house, each and every moment she remained in Caleb's life, would only make it more painful when it was time to say goodbye.

The problem was she didn't know where else to go. She supposed she could stay at her mother's, but she'd never be able to live with herself if she brought danger to her doorstep. There was no way she could battle her allergies to Mr. Whiskers and stay with Layla.

There was no question that she felt the safest right where she was, that she trusted Caleb more than anyone else on the face of the earth to keep her safe. But there was no way to keep her heart safe if she continued to stay here with him.

Her suitcase was packed, but she didn't know

where she would be taking it when she left here. Would she be going home, with Dale or whomever behind bars and the rest of her life stretching before her? Or would she be carrying it someplace else, someplace where Caleb thought she would be safe until this matter was resolved?

Portia jumped as the teakettle began to whistle and moved it off the hot burner. It took her only moments to make her tea and as she carried it into the living room there was a frantic knock on her front door. What the heck? She quickly set the cup on one of the end tables next to the sofa as her heart beat unnaturally fast.

Whoever was at the door couldn't be a threat. Caleb would have never allowed the person to get close enough to knock on the door.

With a horrible sense of foreboding prickling through her she went to the door and turned on the porch light. A woman stood at the door, her features twisted in alarm. "There's a man in your driveway," she yelled through the door. "I think he's hurt." She disappeared from Portia's view.

Was it a trick? Where was Caleb? Her heart beat even faster as she left the door and went to the front window where she could see the driveway.

The beat of her heart felt like it stopped as she saw Caleb's car still in the driveway and his body crumpled next to it. But before she could do anything else, her front door opened and the woman walked inside.

For a moment Portia didn't recognize the woman who held a knife in one hand and Caleb's set of keys in the other. Her pale blue eyes shone with rage. Then recognition struck and she gasped.

Rita Stemple had gained weight and her light brown hair was now a glossy black. Gone was the browbeaten aura that had always clung to her. Instead she looked like an avenging warrior with murder on her mind.

"Hello, Portia. I'm afraid your deputy boyfriend is a bit under the weather. He had an unfortunate encounter with a baseball bat." Rita took a step into the room.

Caleb! Portia's heart crunched in her chest and she fought an overwhelming sense of despair. Was he dead? Had she killed him? She couldn't think about that now, she thought as she focused on the woman in front of her.

"Rita, what's going on? What are you doing here?" A scream was trapped deep inside Portia as terror spiked through her veins but she tried to keep her voice cool and calm.

"Surely you know why I'm here." Rita's fingers tightened on the knife handle as she took another step into the room and dropped the set of keys to the floor. "You ruined my life, Portia, and now it's payback time."

"Rita, I was obligated to report signs of abuse to the authorities," Portia said desperately. "I could have lost my license if I hadn't reported it."

Rita slashed the knife through the air and Portia's fear was so great it felt as if her heart stopped beating for a moment.

"I'm not talking about those damned kids. I never wanted them in the first place. They were Dale's idea. He's the one who wanted them. They needed discipline to keep them in line."

Portia stared at her, stunned as she realized the truth. It hadn't been Dale who had been abusing the Stemple children. It had been Rita. Wrong. They had all gotten it so wrong.

"It's Dale I care about and you screwed it all up for me and him," Rita exclaimed.

"I don't understand. What are you talking about?" Portia asked. *Keep her talking,* she thought to herself. As long as she was talking she wasn't using that wicked-looking knife.

"I was a good wife while Dale was in prison. I visited him when I could. I wrote him every day and never cheated on him. I got a job and sent him money to make his time easier and I waited for him to get out so we could be together again." Rita's voice was raw with emotion. "On the day he was released I went to his parents' house so we could plan our life together and he told me he didn't want me anymore." Angry tears filled her eyes but she didn't loosen her hold on the knife.

"If you hadn't turned us in nobody would have known that he was selling illegal guns, he wouldn't have gone to prison and we would still be together. Now he wants to divorce me and move on with his life without me and it's all your fault."

Without warning she lunged toward Portia. Portia did the only thing she could think of. She grabbed her cup of tea off the end table and threw it in the woman's face.

Rita screeched in outrage as the hot liquid splashed her. She started to raise her hands to wipe her eyes and Portia took the opportunity to kick the knife out of her hand, then Portia shoved past her and tried to get out the front door.

She got halfway there when she was tackled from behind. She sprawled to the floor and quickly turned on her back in an effort to defend herself.

Rita had the knife back in her hand and Portia drew her legs up and kicked in a frenzy, trying to keep the blade from hurting her. One of the kicks connected with Rita's stomach and her breath whooshed out of her on a strangled sob of rage.

She slashed the knife downward and Portia rolled to evade the killing stab. She managed to get to her feet and backed away from Rita, who stood and advanced with a murderous intent.

"There's nobody to save you, Portia. You should

have been dead the night I crawled through your window and tried to strangle you." Rita's chest rose and fell with her labored breathing. "You took away the only thing that mattered to me. It's your fault he doesn't love me anymore. You and your meddling ruined my life. And for that you deserve to die!"

Once again she leaped forward and this time she connected with Portia, the knife ripping across Portia's shoulder even though she stumbled backward to get away.

The pain rippled through her and she released the scream that had been trapped inside her since the moment Rita had appeared in the house.

Reeling with the agony, Portia fell to one knee, but quickly got up as blood poured from the wound and a wave of dizziness cast her sideways on unsteady feet.

This was it, she thought as a sob wrenched from her throat and an overwhelming weariness seeped through her.

She knew Caleb had done his best to protect her, but neither of them had ever considered that they were looking for a woman. None of them had thought about Rita. And now Caleb was dead and Benjamin apparently hadn't heard her scream and there was nobody left to save her.

She pressed her hand to her wound in an attempt to staunch the flow of blood and fell to her knees, unable to summon any more strength to fight back.

Fear mingled with grief, not for her own death, but for Caleb's.

"Please," she whispered and she wasn't sure if it was a plea to let her live or one for death to come quickly.

Rita grinned and the coldness in her eyes intensified. "It's time for revenge," she said.

At that moment the front door burst open and Caleb entered like a raging bull. The side of his head was bloody but his expression was cold and determined. He didn't say a word but rather raised his gun and fired. The bullet hit Rita in the knee and she screamed with agony as she fell to the floor.

Caleb rushed to Portia's side as Benjamin came through the door. "Portia." Caleb gathered her into his arms. "Stay with me," he said.

"I thought you were dead," she said as tears filled her eyes. She reached a hand up and touched the side of his head where blood was still wet and sticky.

"You've always known I have a hard head," he replied.

She closed her eyes, knowing she was safe, that the danger had passed. She was vaguely aware of him calling for an ambulance and then she knew nothing.

Chapter 12

"Maybe you can get a big permanent tattoo to cover the scar," Layla said the next afternoon. She'd arrived at the hospital just a few minutes earlier with a huge bouquet of flowers and a package of temporary tattoos.

Portia had received twelve stitches and was going to be released from the hospital in the next few minutes. "Trust me, after all I've been through a scar is the last thing I'm worried about. Besides, I'm not really the tattoo type of woman."

"I can't believe it was Rita. I can't believe she was the one who was abusing those poor kids." Layla shook her head. "It just goes to show you that you can't know what goes on behind closed doors."

"I'm not sure I want to know what goes on behind closed doors in this town," Portia replied.

"Where's your hero? I figured he'd be here with you," Layla said.

"He was here until about an hour ago and then he got a call from Tom and had to leave. I think Tom needed an official report about what went down last night." Caleb had been right at her side when the doctor had stitched her up, and when he'd insisted that Portia remain hospitalized for blood loss and trauma, Caleb had slept in the chair next to her hospital bed.

They hadn't spoken much except to replay the events that had happened while Caleb was unconscious and Portia had been fighting for her life.

It had felt like the fight with Rita had taken hours, but in reality it had all gone down in a matter of minutes. Benjamin had arrived on the scene to find Caleb getting up, having regained consciousness, and together the two men had burst into the house, praying they weren't too late to save Portia.

"He's supposed to be back here to take me home in an hour or so," she said.

"So what happens now between the two of you?" Layla asked.

"Nothing. I go back to my life and he goes back to his." Portia ignored the pain that sliced through her with her words.

Layla released a dry laugh. "The way I see it neither of you have much of a life going for you. I'd kind of hoped you two would have realized you belong together and there would have been a happily-ever-after kind of ending for you two. It would have given me hope that there might be that kind of an ending for me."

Portia sighed. "To be honest, I'd kind of hoped for that kind of an ending for me and Caleb."

"I knew it!" Layla sat up straighter in her chair. "I knew you were still in love with him," Layla exclaimed triumphantly.

"It doesn't really matter. He's made it clear a million times that he doesn't want a relationship and so it's finished."

"Well, that sucks," Layla said with her usual aplomb.

They both turned as Benjamin came through the door. "I was in the area taking a missing person's report and thought I'd stop in and see how the patient is doing," he said.

"Who's missing?" Layla asked.

"Jennifer Hightower. You know her?" Benjamin asked and both Layla and Portia shook their heads. "She's a twenty-two-year-old and works at the convenience store out on the highway. She didn't come home last night and her roommate hasn't heard from her since she went to work at the store last night."

"She's probably holed up with a boyfriend somewhere," Layla said.

"I hope that's the case," Benjamin replied and then smiled at Portia. "So, how are you doing?"

"I'm fine, ready to get out of here and get back to my house," she said.

"I just thought you'd want to know that Rita had surgery on her knee and is doing fine. She'll be in good shape to spend the rest of her life behind bars." Benjamin stuck his hands in his pockets and rocked back on his heels.

"All's well that ends well," Layla said.

Benjamin nodded. "I had a long talk with Dale Stemple this morning. He wanted me to pass along his sympathies to you. He had no idea Rita was so crazy and he was afraid of letting anyone know he was back in town." Benjamin pulled his hands from his pockets and shrugged. "He seems like a changed man. He told me all he wants to do is get his life back together again and hopefully someday get back custody of his children."

"But wasn't he convicted of child abuse?" Layla asked.

Benjamin shook his head. "No. He agreed to a plea bargain on the illegal weapons charges, but he's always proclaimed his innocence in the abuse of his children."

"But surely he knew it was going on," Portia said.

"The marks that I saw on those kids were evidence of abuse."

"Dale maintains that he was working or out of the house most of the time. He had no idea what was going on with the kids. The only marks he saw on them could be chalked up to regular childhood bruises and bumps."

"And you believe him?" Layla asked dubiously.

Benjamin hesitated a moment and then nodded. "Yeah, I do. Anyway, Portia, I'm glad you're doing okay. It looks like you finally get to return to your life."

"Thank you for everything, Benjamin," she replied.

"I'll just get out of here," he said. "I've got to see if I can figure out where Jennifer Hightower might be." He nodded to both Layla and Portia and then left the room.

"I should get going, too," Layla said as she got up from the chair next to Portia's hospital bed.

"Thanks, Layla. The flowers are beautiful, although I think I'll pass on the tattoos."

Layla walked toward the door and then turned back to her. "Portia, if you really love Caleb, then don't be afraid to fight for him. Tell him how you feel, make him realize the two of you belong together. Love is really the only thing worth fighting for." She turned and left the room.

Portia eased herself out of the bed and went to the

window to look outside as she thought about Layla's parting words.

With her nightmare behind her there was nothing to confuse her feelings where Caleb was concerned. She loved him. It was as simple and as complicated as that. She'd always loved him and she had a feeling she would go to her grave still loving him.

There was no question in her mind now that she had misjudged him years ago, that she'd made the biggest mistake of her life when she'd broken up with him.

And she believed with all her heart, all her soul, that he loved her, too. But could she get beneath the defenses he'd erected around his heart? Could she make him see that they deserved a second chance to find happiness together?

Love is really the only thing worth fighting for. Layla's words were still playing in her head a few minutes later when Caleb walked into the room.

"Hey, how are you doing?"

She turned from the window and smiled at him. "Pretty good. I'm ready to get out of here, that's for sure."

"I just spoke to the doctor and he said you've been released." He walked over and stood in front of her and he took her chin between his fingers and tilted her head upward. "Yes, you definitely look better than you did last night. Your color is back and your eyes are shining bright."

With love, she wanted to say, but she didn't. She didn't want to talk to him about her feelings here in the middle of a hospital room, where anyone could walk in and interrupt what she wanted, what she needed to say.

"I'm just ready to go home," she said as he dropped his hand from her chin.

"Then let's get out of here." He picked up the vase of flowers that Layla had brought and together they left the room.

Thankfully one of the nurses had provided a clean T-shirt for Portia to wear home. The one she'd worn the night before had been ruined, torn by the knife and bloodied by the wound.

They left the hospital and got into Caleb's car. She noticed her suitcase was in the backseat. He'd made sure that she'd have no reason to go back to his house. Her heart sank.

"I talked to Wally this morning down at the garage and he said your car is finished. He'll have it delivered to your house sometime this afternoon so you won't have to go without wheels," Caleb said as he started the engine.

"Great. I think I'll take the next couple of days and finish painting the inside of the day care before I have the children come back. A fresh start sounds like a wonderful idea." She glanced at him, wondering if he had any idea how badly she wanted a fresh start with him.

He kept his gaze focused on the road, apparently completely unaware of the war going on in her heart. Should she tell him how she felt? Or was it smarter just to tell him goodbye and never let him know the depth of her love for him? Could she live with her regrets of what might have been if she didn't say anything at all?

She wouldn't die without him in her life. She'd go on to find happiness eventually, but she would always remember the deputy with the dark eyes and that charming half grin, the boy who'd taken her virginity and the man who had stolen her heart.

By the time they reached her house she knew she had to speak what was in her heart. As she carried the flowers, Caleb grabbed her suitcase from the back and together they walked to her front door.

She unlocked the door and went inside, nervous tension coiling tight in the pit of her stomach. She walked through the living room to the kitchen, aware of him following close behind her.

She placed the vase on the counter and then turned to look at him and in that moment she knew she was going to tell him everything that was inside her. Layla was right, this kind of love was definitely worth fighting for.

"Caleb." Her throat was painfully dry and she wasn't sure where to begin.

"Portia," he replied with a smile. He dropped her suitcase to the floor. "I'm glad this is all over for you, that your life will return to normal again and you don't have to be afraid anymore. So I guess this is goodbye." His eyes were dark and unreadable.

"It doesn't have to be." She took a step toward him, her legs suddenly feeling wobbly with nerves. "I'm in love with you, Caleb. I want a second chance. I think we belong together."

She paused, watching his features intently. Nothing changed. It was as if he hadn't heard her. She took another step closer to him, now standing close enough to smell his familiar scent, to feel his body heat radiating over her.

"Caleb, say something. I'm baring my heart here." Tears began to burn her eyes. "I love you. I've always loved you and I want to spend my life with you. You're the one, Caleb. The one I want to share my hopes with, the one I want to build dreams with, you're the one I want for the rest of my life."

For just a quicksilver moment a longing flashed in his eyes, but it was gone as quickly as it had appeared. "Portia, I told you all along that I'm not looking for a relationship." His gaze couldn't hold hers and instead he stared down at the floor. "I'm sorry if I somehow led you on."

"You love me, Caleb. I know you do," she exclaimed with fervor. "For God's sake, give us our chance to get it right. Let me into your life like I know I'm already in your heart."

His gaze shot back to her but instead of seeing joy

in the depths of his eyes, she saw despair as he took a step backward. "Don't do this, Portia. Don't make it more difficult than it already is."

"I'm not trying to be difficult," she protested. "I'm trying to make you see that we belong together."

He shook his head and took another step back from her. "We don't belong together. We had our chance and we blew it. I just don't want to put my heart on the line ever again."

She stared at him in stunned surprise. "You know what I think, Caleb? I think I hurt you and I'll always be sorry for that. But I think Laura devastated you."

She paused and fought back her tears. "I was always secretly afraid that I'd become like my mother, afraid to look for happiness, afraid of being hurt again. Caleb, if you embrace your bitterness and keep love out of your life forever then you're going to wind up like her, cold and alone."

He jammed his hands into his pockets. "I did what I promised I'd do. I got you your life back and you aren't in danger anymore. I can't do anything else for you, Portia."

"You mean you won't do anything more for me," she exclaimed as tears fell from her eyes. "Because you're afraid."

"You think what you want. Find a good man, Portia. Get married and have all those babies you always wanted. I'll see you around." He whirled on his heels and strode out of the room.

A moment later she heard the front door close and knew he was gone. Gone in a way he'd never been gone before. A tight band squeezed her chest in a pain she'd never felt. She recognized it as complete and utter heartbreak and the shattering of dreams never realized.

She sank down at a chair at the table and laid her head in her arms and cried for everything that might have been and now would never be.

"Joey, we don't put our beans up our nose," Portia said as she used a napkin to wipe the baked beans off the four-year-old's nostrils.

"How come?" he asked.

"Because beans don't like noses, beans like mouths," she replied and kissed his forehead before moving to the next child who needed a kiss, a face wipe or help with their lunch.

It had been three days since Caleb had walked out of her kitchen and not looked back. For the first two days Portia had lost herself in finishing the painting of the interior of the day care and getting things ready to welcome back the children.

They had returned yesterday and the last two days had been filled with happy kisses, fierce hugs and enough laughter to keep heartache at bay, at least during the day.

It was only after the kids left and she'd finished eating dinner that the house resounded with a silence that was deafening and the heartbreak became so overwhelming she could scarcely stand it.

It might have been easier if she believed that Caleb didn't love her, if she was certain that he had cast her out of his life because he didn't want her. But she didn't believe that and that was as heartbreaking as anything.

She knew eventually the pain would lessen, that there might come a time when she would think about Caleb and not feel the excruciating arrow of pain through her heart. But she was a long way from that point in time at the moment.

"You okay?" Melody pulled Portia from her thoughts.

"Fine." Portia smiled at the assistant who had been a godsend through the entire ordeal. "I'm just glad to have the kids back."

"They're all thrilled to be back here," Melody replied. "Every day they were at my house they asked when they could come back here and be with Ms. Portia."

Portia's heart expanded with love for all of the children who were in her care. "You need to have some babies of your own, Portia," Melody said.

"Maybe someday," Portia said wistfully. "And now we'd better get the rest of the lunch mess cleaned up before Joey actually does manage to get a leftover bean up his nose."

The rest of the afternoon passed all too quickly and then it was time for the parents to arrive to pick up their children. As always, when the last child left, Portia felt as if a little piece of her heart had been ripped away.

The silence in the day-care center heralded in thoughts of Caleb. As she straightened books and put toys away, her head filled with thoughts of the man who'd refused to accept her love, who had refused to embrace his own love for her.

Even if he didn't want a future with her, she hoped that someday he could put aside his bitterness and find a life partner, some woman he would love to distraction. The thought of him spending the rest of his life alone made her ache for him.

In the three days that had passed since she'd last seen him, had he thought of her? Did he have any regret in his heart?

She hadn't ventured into town, had been afraid that she might catch a glimpse of him, that she might have to make friendly conversation if they met on the street and she just wasn't ready to do that. Her pain was still too fresh, too raw.

Eventually they would run into each other at a town function or in the grocery store. Eventually she would have to smile and pretend that the mere sight of him didn't break her heart all over again.

She straightened a stack of coloring books and then turned to leave. She gasped as she saw the object of her thoughts standing in the doorway.

"Hi, Portia," he said.

"Caleb." Her heart leaped into her throat at the sight of him. He was clad in a pair of worn jeans that hugged the length of his legs and a white T-shirt that stretched taut across his broad shoulders. He looked strong and sexy and Portia wanted to order him away and throw herself in his arms at same time.

"You're off duty today?" she asked, pleased that her voice sounded normal and not strained with the tension that gripped her.

"On vacation," he replied. He took a step into the room and looked around. "The new paint looks nice, bright and cheerful."

"Thanks. What are you doing here, Caleb? I'm sure you didn't come here just to check out the new paint," she said, a hint of irritation in her voice. If he thought they could be friends now, he was dead wrong. She couldn't be friends with a man she loved, a man who refused to admit he loved her.

He raked a hand through his hair, causing that charming curl to droop across his forehead. He focused his gaze on her and in the depths of his brown eyes she saw a hint of vulnerability.

"I've tried, Portia. For the last three days I've tried hard to convince myself that I did the right thing in walking away from you. I tried to tell myself that

I was the kind of man who could live alone, that I could wrap my bitterness around me and that that was all I needed to keep me warm, but I was wrong."

He made no move toward her and she remained rooted in place, afraid to hope, afraid to believe the reason he might be here. "You're right. You hurt me years ago when you didn't believe me, when you thought I'd cheated on you. And you're right again, Laura made me leery of ever trusting a woman again."

He drew a deep breath and cast his gaze out the nearby window. "I didn't want to love you, Portia. I thought what we had was just a physical attraction. I thought what I felt for you was nothing more than leftover emotions from the past. I thought I was done with love, but I was wrong."

Once again he looked at her and in his eyes was a softness, a deep yearning that made Portia catch her breath. He walked over to where she stood and took her chin between his thumb and finger.

"When we were sophomores in high school I thought you were the cutest girl I'd ever seen. When we were juniors you were not only my best friend, but the girl I wanted to spend all my time with, and when we were seniors I not only wanted you with a man's passion, but I realized how much I loved you, as well. And as a woman you absolutely take my breath away."

He dropped his hand from her face but didn't

move away from her. "I made you a promise a long time ago. I promised to be true to you and love you forever. I didn't break that promise years ago and I don't intend to break that promise in the future."

His words created a song in her heart, a happiness that filled her heart to capacity. "Caleb Grayson, if you don't take me in your arms this minute I'm going to die."

He smiled then, that sexy beautiful grin that never failed to light a fire in her. He pulled her against him and the kiss they shared held all the passion of youth, the joy of forgiveness and a love that she knew would last until the end of time.

When the kiss ended he looked down at her. "You're the one for me, Portia. The only one I want to wake up to in the morning, the only one I want to hold in my arms through the night. I want you to marry me, Portia."

"Yes," she said. "Yes, I want that, too. We'll get it right this time, Caleb."

"It is right," he replied, his eyes shining with promise and the love she'd known burned deep in his heart.

She placed a hand on his cheek. "I want to have your baby, Caleb."

He tightened his arms around her and gazed at her with a hunger that nearly stole her breath away. "I want that. I want you and marriage and babies."

"You already have me. It will take a while to

arrange for a marriage, but we could start working on that baby thing right away," she said.

His eyes lit with a flame that shot fire through Portia's veins. "What are we waiting for?" He took her by the hand and led her out of the day care and toward her house, to the happily-ever-after they were meant to share.

Epilogue

Brittany Grayson awoke with a gasp. She sat up on the cot and an overwhelming despair swept through her. Waking was the worst, when she left happy dreams of family and safety and realized the tiny cell wasn't a nightmare, but rather her reality.

As always when she first awakened she studied her surroundings, looking for any weakness that might provide an escape.

The barn had been transformed into a jail, with five cells complete with strong iron bars. Each cell not only had a bed, but also stainless-steel bathroom fixtures.

The interior of the structure had been soundproofed and in the first couple of days after she'd slept off whatever drugs she'd been given, she had screamed herself hoarse, but nobody had heard her cries.

She had no idea who her captor was or what he intended to do with her. All she knew was that she'd lost track of the days she'd been here, he wasn't feeding her enough to keep her strong and she was in terrible trouble.

She closed her eyes for a moment and summoned a mental picture of her brothers. Tom with his quiet confidence, Jacob with haunting secrets that darkened his eyes, Benjamin with his easygoing personality and ready smile and finally Caleb with the big heart that he tried to hide. Her heart ached with the need to be with them.

They would be frantic. They would be looking for her, but she didn't even know where she was, didn't know if she was still in the small town of Black Rock. She didn't even know if she was still in the state of Kansas. For all she knew she could be hundreds, thousands of miles away from her home.

Tears burned but she bit them back, refusing to cry. She'd already cried buckets full of tears and crying wasn't going to get her out of here.

The last thing she remembered before awakening in this cell was being in her car and getting ready for a night out at Harley's. She had a little crush on one of the bartenders and had been looking forward to spending the evening in a little harmless flirting.

She'd put the key in the ignition and an arm

had come from the backseat and around her neck, pinning her back to the seat while a hand had pressed a noxious-smelling rag to her face.

Stupid. She'd been so stupid. She'd left her car doors unlocked and when she'd gotten into the car she hadn't thought to check the backseat.

She was a deputy, for God's sake, and she hadn't practiced the first rules of safety. And now she was in trouble, terrible trouble.

She heard the sound of a man's whistling and it shot terror through her. He was coming! Was this the time he would kill her?

She stood from the cot as the whistling grew louder and then the outer door opened and he stepped inside. As always he wore a ski mask to hide his features. What wasn't usual was that he carried an unconscious red-haired girl in his arms.

"Good morning, Brittany." He had a pleasant voice that Brittany thought sounded vaguely familiar but she couldn't place.

He opened the door to the cell next to Brittany's and laid the young woman on the cot. Brittany saw her face and recognized her. Jennifer Hightower. She worked at the convenience store where Brittany often stopped for a cup of coffee on the go.

"What are you doing? Let her go!" Brittany grabbed the steel bars of her enclosure. "You creep! You pervert!"

"Ah, sticks and stones..." He stepped out of

Jennifer's cell and locked the door. "You should be happy. For you, she's company and for me, she's an audience."

"An audience?" Brittany's heart thundered in her chest.

"I do my best work when I have an audience." He pointed to the empty cells. "When I have those full, then the games will begin." He laughed, a horrifying sound of anticipation. "Unfortunately, you probably won't find the game as fun as I will."

He laughed again and then began to whistle as he left the barn and closed the door behind him. A wash of terror swept over Brittany as she sank back down on the cot.

Glancing over at the unconscious woman in the cell next to her, her mind raced. They had to still be close to Black Rock for him to have abducted Jennifer and brought her here.

Impotent anger balled her hands into fists. It was her duty as a deputy to protect and serve the people of Black Rock, but she couldn't help Jennifer. She couldn't even help herself.

She cried out her brothers' names in her head, willing them to find her, to save her. She knew in the very depths of her being that if they didn't find her before those other cells were filled with women, then she would never see them again.

* * * * *

COMING NEXT MONTH

Available July 27, 2010

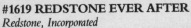

ROMANTIC SUSPENSE

REQUEST YOUR FREE BOOKS!

2 FREE NOVELS PLUS 2 FREE GIFTS!

Silhouette

ROMANTIC SUSPENSE

Sparked by Danger, Fueled by Passion.

YES! Please send me 2 FREE Silhouette® Romantic Suspense novels and my 2 FREE gifts (gifts are worth about $10). After receiving them, if I don't wish to receive any more books, I can return the shipping statement marked "cancel." If I don't cancel, I will receive 4 brand-new novels every month and be billed just $4.24 per book in the U.S. or $4.99 per book in Canada. That's a saving of 15% off the cover price! It's quite a bargain! Shipping and handling is just 50¢ per book.* I understand that accepting the 2 free books and gifts places me under no obligation to buy anything. I can always return a shipment and cancel at any time. Even if I never buy another book from Silhouette, the two free books and gifts are mine to keep forever.

240/340 SDN E5Q4

Name _____ (PLEASE PRINT) _____

Address _____ Apt. # _____

City _____ State/Prov. _____ Zip/Postal Code _____

Signature (if under 18, a parent or guardian must sign)

Mail to the Silhouette Reader Service:

IN U.S.A.: P.O. Box 1867, Buffalo, NY 14240-1867
IN CANADA: P.O. Box 609, Fort Erie, Ontario L2A 5X3

Not valid for current subscribers to Silhouette Romantic Suspense books.

Want to try two free books from another line?
Call 1-800-873-8635 or visit www.morefreebooks.com.

* Terms and prices subject to change without notice. Prices do not include applicable taxes. N.Y. residents add applicable sales tax. Canadian residents will be charged applicable provincial taxes and GST. Offer not valid in Quebec. This offer is limited to one order per household. All orders subject to approval. Credit or debit balances in a customer's account(s) may be offset by any other outstanding balance owed by or to the customer. Please allow 4 to 6 weeks for delivery. Offer available while quantities last.

Your Privacy: Silhouette is committed to protecting your privacy. Our Privacy Policy is available online at www.eHarlequin.com or upon request from the Reader Service. From time to time we make our lists of customers available to reputable third parties who may have a product or service of interest to you. If you would prefer we not share your name and address, please check here. ☐

Help us get it right—We strive for accurate, respectful and relevant communications. To clarify or modify your communication preferences, visit us at www.ReaderService.com/consumerschoice.

SRS10R

HARLEQUIN®

A *Romance*

FOR EVERY MOOD™

Spotlight on

Heart & Home

Heartwarming romances
where love can happen
right when you least expect it.

See the next page to enjoy a sneak peek
from Harlequin® American Romance®,
a Heart and Home series.

Five hunky Texas single fathers—five stories from Cathy Gillen Thacker's LONE STAR DADS *miniseries. Here's an excerpt from the latest, THE MOMMY PROPOSAL from Harlequin American Romance.*

"I hear you work miracles," Nate Hutchinson drawled. Brooke Mitchell had just stepped into his lavishly appointed office in downtown Fort Worth, Texas.

"Sometimes, I do." Brooke smiled and took the sexy financier's hand in hers, shook it briefly.

"Good." Nate looked her straight in the eye. "Because I'm in need of a home makeover—fast. The son of an old friend is coming to live with me."

She was still tingling from the feel of his warm palm. "Temporarily or permanently?"

"If all goes according to plan, I'll adopt Landry by summer's end."

Brooke had heard the founder of Nate Hutchinson Financial Services was eligible, wealthy and generous to a fault. She hadn't known he was in the market for a family, but she supposed she shouldn't be surprised. But Brooke had figured a man as successful and handsome as Nate would want one the old-fashioned way. *Not that this was any of her business...*

"So what's the child like?" she asked crisply, trying not to think how the marine-blue of Nate's dress shirt deepened the hue of his eyes.

"I don't know." Nate took a seat behind his massive antique mahogany desk. He relaxed against the smooth leather of the chair. "I've never met him."

"Yet you've invited this kid to live with you permanently?"

"It's complicated. But I'm sure it's going to be fine."

Obviously Nate Hutchinson knew as little about teenage

boys as he did about decorating. But that wasn't her problem.
Finding a way to do the assignment without getting the least
bit emotionally involved was.

Find out how a young boy brings Nate and Brooke
together in THE MOMMY PROPOSAL,
coming August 2010 from Harlequin American Romance.

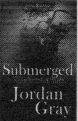

THE HEAT IS ON

by

Jill Shalvis

The attraction between Bella and
Detective Madden is undeniable.
But can a few wild encounters
turn into love?

Don't miss this hot read.

*Available in August
where books are sold.*

red-hot reads

www.eHarlequin.com

HB79562